American Events

THE NEGRO BASEBALL LEAGUES

David K. Fremon

New Discovery Books
New York

Maxwell Macmillan Canada
Toronto

Maxwell Macmillan International
New York Oxford Singapore Sydney

S0-CFM-428

Book design: Deborah Fillion
All photos courtesy of the National Baseball Library & Archive, Cooperstown, N.Y.

New Discovery Books
Macmillan Publishing Company
866 Third Avenue
New York, NY 10022

Maxwell Macmillan Canada, Inc.
1200 Eglinton Avenue East
Suite 200
Don Mills, Ontario M3C 3N1

Macmillan Publishing Company is part of the Maxwell Communication Group of Companies.

First Edition

Printed in the United States

10 9 8 7 6 5 4 3 2 1

Library of Congress Cataloging-in-Publication Data

Fremon, David K.
    The Negro baseball leagues / by David Fremon. — 1st ed.
      p. cm. — (American events)
    Includes bibliographical references (p.).
    ISBN 0-02-735695-7
    1. Negro leagues—History—Juvenile literature. 2. Baseball—United States—History—Juvenile literature. 3. Afro-American baseball players—Juvenile literature. I. Title. II. Series.
    GV863.A1F74 1994
    796.357'0973—dc20   94-2389
    Summary: The history of the various Negro-league baseball teams, which existed from 1920–1960.

0-382-24730-2 (pbk.)

To Palomela, who was a big, big help.

Roy Campanella, one of the many players to get a start in the Negro leagues, tags a runner out.

CONTENTS

1 ★ ORGANIZED BUT NOT RECOGNIZED   7

2 ★ "GET THAT NIGGER OFF THE FIELD!"   11

3 ★ RUBE FOSTER AND THE NEGRO
      NATIONAL LEAGUE   21

4 ★ LIFE ON THE ROAD—
      "YOU GOT USED TO IT"   31

5 ★ SATCH   41

6 ★ A GALAXY OF STARS   47

7 ★ MONARCHS, GRAYS, AND CRAWFORDS   55

8 ★ "THEY CONSIDERED US EQUALS"   61

9 ★ THE ROAD TO INTEGRATION   69

10 ★ "WE PAVED THE WAY"   81

   ★ NOTES   91

   ★ FOR FURTHER READING   94

   ★ INDEX   96

Jackie Robinson waves to fans outside the Dodgers clubhouse.

Chapter 1

ORGANIZED BUT NOT RECOGNIZED

When Jackie Robinson stepped up to the plate on April 18, 1946, the prayers of millions of Americans went with him. Jack Roosevelt Robinson, second baseman for the minor-league Montreal Royals, was the first black player to appear in a major- or minor-league baseball game in nearly 60 years. If he played well, other black players might soon find their way into the major and minor leagues. If he failed, the course of baseball integration might be set back for years.

His first time at bat, Robinson grounded out weakly. Then he exploded. Robinson ended his first minor-league game with a home run and three other hits. He stole two bases, including home, and his aggressive baserunning led to a pitcher's balk that scored another run.

Robinson's debut marked the beginning of integration in organized major- and minor-league baseball, which had been closed to blacks for decades. But it also marked the beginning of the end for the Negro leagues, all-black professional leagues that had formed because white owners had kept black players out of major- and minor-league baseball.

Professional baseball, to use the terminology of an 1896 U.S. Supreme Court case, was "separate but equal," except that it was not equal at all. White major-league baseball players received high salaries, stayed at the best hotels, ate in the top restaurants, and rode the finest trains from city to city. Negro-league players played many more games for far less money, traveled in dilapidated buses or crowded cars, and stayed in black-only hotels—if they could find any accommodations at all.

Despite many hardships, Negro leaguers played exciting, aggressive baseball that won praise even from white fans. The innovations of black players and Negro-league teams forever changed the face of the game. Night baseball, batting helmets, shin guards, the hit-and-run play, and the feetfirst slide—all originated with black players and Negro-league teams.

Only the most bigoted of fans could deny that the top black stars were equal if not superior to the best white players. Even though they never played an inning of major-league ball, Josh Gibson, Buck Leonard, Oscar Charleston, and many others gained the respect and admiration of the major-league stars they faced in barnstorming matches, in which black and white players displayed their talents against one another in exhibition games.

But while major-league baseball stars were known throughout the country by blacks and whites alike, black stars remained unknown to most white fans. Monte Irvin, who starred with the Negro-league Newark Eagles and later with the major-league New York Giants, said:

> Suppose Willie Mays had never had a chance to play in the big leagues, then I were to come to you and try to tell you about Willie Mays. This is the way it was with Cool Papa Bell. This is the way it was with Buck Leonard. Just a fantastic hitter. With Oscar Charleston, who they say was just as good as Willie—or *better*. But very few people got to see him play.
>
> If they could have removed the Jim Crow barrier even just ten years earlier, there would've been twenty to twenty-five men they could've taken right into major league clubs and they'd have been potential Hall of Famers. There were *that* many.[1]

The Kansas City Monarchs in a team photo after winning the first Negro League World Series in 1924

Willie Mays, the Giants center fielder who is considered by many the greatest player in major-league history, started his career with the Birmingham Black Barons. He acknowledged the role that Negro-league baseball played in his development: "The major leagues were very easy for me. I learned baseball the hard way; the Negro leagues made me."[2]

For black Americans, the Negro leagues were more than gatherings of ballplayers. Black baseball teams were among the largest black-owned businesses in the country. They provided money and pride at a time when much of white America was unwilling to give blacks either.

Despite the accomplishments of the Negro leagues, some refused to give them ample credit. Kenesaw Mountain Landis, the baseball commissioner whose stubbornness kept baseball segregated, sneered at the Negro leagues and said, "They're not organized." First base star Buck Leonard replied, "We were organized. We just weren't recognized."[3]

Chapter 2

"GET THAT NIGGER OFF THE FIELD!"

General Robert E. Lee surrendered to General Ulysses S. Grant at Appomattox, Virginia, in 1865, ending the Civil War. Soon slavery was officially outlawed everywhere in the United States. Blacks were free.

However, newly freed black Americans soon discovered that freedom did not necessarily mean equality. Southerners hated and resented the men and women who had been their slaves. Many northerners disliked the institution of slavery but nonetheless considered blacks inferior. Northern and southern whites alike kept blacks out of many of their institutions. More often than not, colleges, businesses, and social organizations closed their doors to blacks.

Freedom for the slaves was not the only change in American society brought about by the Civil War. Between battles, northern troops had relaxed by playing the newly created game of baseball. Captured Confederate soldiers learned the game and brought it home to the South. Soon every city, small town, farm village, and mining camp in the United States had one or more baseball teams. Blacks as well as whites enjoyed the game.

The National Association of Base Ball Players formed in 1867 to establish playing rules for its 100 member clubs. Unfortunately, racial fairness played no part in this organization. The 237 delegates to the nominating committee unanimously called for the exclusion "of any club which may be composed of one or more colored persons."[1]

The Cincinnatti Red Stockings

Baseball's popularity led to the formation of the first all-professional team, the Cincinnati Red Stockings, in 1869. The team's success spawned the first all-professional major league, the National Association of Professional Baseball Players, two years later. Professional minor leagues followed. The National Association, unlike its predecessor, did not have a formal rule barring black players. Instead it operated under a "gentlemen's agreement" in which all team owners silently promised to keep blacks off their rosters.

A new league, the National League, replaced the National Association in 1876. It also abided by the "gentlemen's agreement." The league's most successful franchise was the Chicago White Stockings, headed by manager and first baseman Adrian "Cap" Anson.

Tradition calls the quiet town of Cooperstown, New York, the birthplace of baseball. Although few believe baseball was invented there, Cooperstown did produce a notable native son—John "Bud" Fowler, the first black professional ballplayer of the 19th century. Fowler played his first pro game in 1872 and continued for more than 20 years. Although he never appeared in the majors, he was considered one of the best second basemen in the country.

While Fowler was appearing wherever he could get a paycheck, Moses Fleetwood Walker was studying French, Greek, philosophy, and engineering at Oberlin College, in Ohio. The prestigious school did not have a baseball team until Walker's final year. The black student starred as a batter and catcher for Oberlin's team. Walker's brother Weldy Wilburforce Walker played right field. After leaving Oberlin, "Fleet" Walker turned professional. In 1883 he joined the Toledo Blue Stockings of the Northwestern League, which did not abide by the "gentlemen's agreement," and helped bring the team a championship.

Like other minor-league teams of the time, Toledo occasionally played exhibitions against major-league clubs. One such match was to take place against Anson's White Stockings.

During his playing career, Cap Anson was renowned as an outstanding and honorable baseball man. Today he is remembered mainly as a racist. Anson hated black people, especially black baseball players.

Before the game, a White Stockings official wrote to Toledo manager C. H. Morton telling him not to play the team's "colored man."[2] Morton was not about to take orders from a bigot. He put Walker in right field and reminded Anson that he would forfeit the game and $100 if he refused to play the game. A grumbling Anson took the field.

Toledo joined the American Association, then a major league, in 1884, and Fleet Walker became the first black major leaguer. He was a better-than-average player, although injuries limited his 1884 effectiveness. Weldy

Moses Fleetwood Walker (back row center) poses with the International League's Kedkuk, Iowa, team in 1885.

Walker became the second black big leaguer; he played a few games in the outfield for Toledo at the end of the season.

His Toledo teammates showed no resentment toward Fleet Walker. Fans likewise tolerated him, except in two southern cities. When Louisville fans booed him, Toledo fans in turn booed the Louisville players. Toledo's team received a threatening letter signed by people who claimed to be players with the Richmond team, although no one with those names played for Richmond. Fleet Walker was released because of injuries that September but was still admired by fans and teammates. *Sporting Life*'s Toledo reporter wrote, "To his fine work last year much of the success of the Toledo Club was due, as none will deny. This year, however, he has been extremely unfortunate, having met with several accidents which kept him disabled a large part of the time. . . . By his fine, gentlemanly deportment, he made hosts of friends."[3]

Toledo's team folded after the 1884 season, and Walker never returned to the majors. Instead he found a spot with the newly formed International League. By now, other blacks were playing professional ball, including a 19-year-old infielder named Sol White who would later become a noted baseball historian. Frank Grant, a second baseman, was perhaps the best of all of them. *Sporting Life*'s Buffalo writer called him "the best all-around player Buffalo ever had,"[4] from a team that included three future Baseball Hall of Famers. George Stovey, a black Canadian, became known as one of baseball's most effective left-handed pitchers. He won 34 games for Newark's International League team in 1887.

But effectiveness did not always translate into respect from other players. Grant led his league in home runs and batting average in 1887, yet his teammates refused to pose with him in the team photo. Pitcher Tony Mullane said of Walker, "He was the best catcher I ever worked with, but I disliked a Negro, and whenever I had to pitch to him, I used anything I wanted without looking at his signals."[5]

Opponents' racism sometimes led to a physical danger for black players, and they used their ingenuity to protect themselves. Fowler and Grant both played second base, the position where a fielder is most vulnerable to enemy base runners. Each has been credited with being the first player to use shin guards to avoid attacks from opponents' spikes. Grant invented the feetfirst slide, to avoid being tagged on the head by enemy infielders, and drew many bases on balls, because opposing pitchers often threw at his head.

Newark's Little Giants, with George Stovey on the roster, scheduled an 1887 exhibition game with Cap Anson's White Stockings. This time, the bigoted Anson would not be stopped. He pointed at the pitcher and shouted, "Get that nigger off the field!"[6] The Newark manager, who lacked

Morton's backbone, obeyed Anson's demand. A reporter for *Sporting Life* referred to the incident as "the first time in baseball history the color line had been drawn."[7]

Anson's influence extended beyond his own diamond. When New York Giants manager John Montgomery Ward planned to sign Stovey, Anson raised a clamor and Ward backed off.

Even though Anson was influential, his demands would have been ignored had others not shared his views. At the same time Anson forced Stovey off the field, the owners in the International League were doing the same to other black players. *Sporting Life* reported that "several representatives declared

Cap Anson

that many of the best players in the League were anxious to leave on account of the colored element, and the board finally directed Secretary White to approve no more contracts with colored men."[8] Blacks in the league at the time could continue playing, but no new ones could be signed.

Lessened opportunities for black players in white-controlled leagues did not mean the end of black baseball. Instead black players formed their own teams.

A group of waiters from a Babylon, Long Island, hotel created the first

The Cuban Giants

all-black professional team. They were hired for their ballplaying rather than tray-carrying skills. The waiters called themselves the Cuban Giants—*Giants* because the New York Giants were a dominant National League team and *Cuban* because Cubans were not subjected to as much prejudice as were blacks. On the field they spoke gibberish they hoped fans would interpret as Spanish. The Cuban Giants defeated most rivals, including the American Association's Cincinnati Red Stockings. Their success led to the formation of many other black teams, most of which employed *Cuban* or *Giants* in their name: the Cuban X Giants, Chicago Columbia Giants, Chicago Unions, Philadelphia Giants, and Brooklyn Royal Giants. Several black teams formed a league in 1887, a disorganized outfit that lasted less than a month.

Fleet Walker was released by Syracuse after 1889, becoming the last black player in the International League. White leagues, meanwhile, followed the IL's lead in barring black players. One by one, the black players left for all-black teams or quit playing baseball altogether. At one time or another, about 60 black players had played on organized baseball teams in the 19th century. By 1898 there were none.

The segregation appearing in baseball was also being mirrored in American society. A historic 1896 U.S. Supreme Court case, *Plessy v. Ferguson,* ruled that states could pass "Jim Crow" laws requiring separate public facilities for whites and "coloreds." These laws meant exclusion of blacks from hotels, restaurants, and other facilities, particularly in the South.

The major leagues still had no written rule against hiring black players, although no owner was willing to break the long-standing "gentlemen's agreement." But John McGraw, manager of the new American League's Baltimore Orioles, was more interested in winning pennants than enforcing segregation.

Charlie Grant, an outstanding black infielder with the Chicago Columbia Giants, was working as a busboy at a Hot Springs, Arkansas, hotel and playing baseball. McGraw, at Hot Springs for spring training, immediately wanted Grant for the Orioles. He knew he had no chance to sign Grant under normal circumstances, so he came up with a plan. Looking at a hotel map, he noticed Tokohoma Creek and borrowed the name. Charlie Grant would become Charlie Tokohoma, a Cherokee Indian. Since baseball teams were not prohibited from signing Native Americans, McGraw tried to employ the ruse to sign the light-skinned Grant.

Sporting News called Tokohoma "a phenomenal fielder . . . moreover, a good batter."[9] But the disguise failed to fool Chicago White Sox owner Charles Comiskey, who had heard of Grant. Proud black fans cheered loudly for Grant at a preseason game. Comiskey then told a sportswriter, "Somebody told me this Cherokee of McGraw's is really Grant, the crack Negro second baseman, fixed up with war paint and a bunch of feathers."[10]

McGraw soon gave up the "Charlie Tokohoma" charade, and Grant returned to the Columbia Giants. McGraw openly admired other black stars but made no further attempts to sign them. Nor did any other major leaguer for nearly half a century. Sol White, the star second baseman who wrote a history of black baseball in 1906, commented, "Nowhere in American Life is the color line more firmly drawn than in baseball."[11]

Charlie Grant

Chapter 3

RUBE FOSTER AND THE NEGRO NATIONAL LEAGUE

John McGraw might not have been able to hire a black baseball player, but he still found a way to utilize black talent. McGraw, who had become manager of the New York Giants, asked a black pitcher to work with young hurlers Christy Mathewson and Joe McGinnity in early 1903. The tutoring obviously helped. Mathewson jumped from 14 wins in 1902 to 30 in 1903. McGinnity won 31 games, and the Giants jumped from last place to second. They would win pennants in 1904 and 1905.

McGraw's instructor was no ordinary pitcher. In fact, he was one of the most extraordinary people in baseball history, Andrew "Rube" Foster. Combine the talents of Mathewson, McGraw, American League founder Byron "Ban" Johnson, and iron-willed Commissioner Kenesaw Mountain Landis—that was Foster, the father of black baseball.

At only 23, Foster, ace of the Philadelphia Stars, was already a pitching legend when he gave the Giants their pitching lessons. In 1902 his searing fastball and nasty screwball defeated Philadelphia Athletics star Rube Waddell in an exhibition game, and he proudly carried the nickname Rube for the rest of his life. And despite his age, Rube Foster was no amateur. Pittsburgh Pirates star Honus Wagner called Foster "the smartest pitcher I have ever seen in all my years of baseball."[1]

In 1907 Foster moved from the Stars to Chicago's Leland Giants. He convinced stars such as shortstop John Henry Lloyd and second baseman

Rube Foster

Grant "Home Run" Johnson to go with him. He also convinced owner Frank Leland to let him negotiate game fees. Thereafter, the Giants always received at least 50 percent of the gate profits for their games.

The World Series champion Chicago Cubs faced the Leland Giants in a three-game series in 1908. The Cubs won all three games, although according to an influential black newspaper, the *Chicago Defender*, "Fans made fun at the way officials deliberately favored the Cubs just enough to assure victory."[2] Two years later Foster pitched and managed the Leland Giants to an incredible 123–6 record.

Rube Foster parted from the Leland Giants after 1910 to form his own team. With John Schorling, the son-in-law of White Sox owner Charles Comiskey, he leased the White Sox's old ballpark and formed the Chicago American Giants, one of the greatest teams in baseball history.

Opponents often called the American Giants "racehorses" because of their team speed. Foster demanded that his players go for an extra base on singles and doubles. He also worked his players to become the game's best bunters. When he threw a hat onto the infield, the player had to be able to bunt into that hat. He invented the hit-and-run play. With a fast runner on first base, the batter would bunt the ball to third. The runner, moving with the pitch, would be past second by the time the ball reached the bat and at third when the third baseman threw the ball to first. If any of the infielders made a mistake, the runner could score. White major-league managers often attended Foster's games to learn his tactics.

Foster would do virtually anything to win a ball game. Sometimes visiting teams found Chicago infields "drowned"—drenched with water—to slow up bunts so they took longer to get to infielders, which helped give fleet American Giants singles. On other occasions, when slugging opposition teams came to town, baseballs were frozen overnight before the game, making it all but impossible to hit them out of the park. St. Louis Stars outfielder James "Cool Papa" Bell claimed Foster dug a small ridge in the foul lines to prevent balls from rolling over and help make his team's bunts fair balls.[3]

Foster directed games from the bench, waving his ever-present pipe in what appeared to be signals. As often as not, however, the pipe was a decoy. While opposing managers watched Foster and tried to intercept his signals, someone on the bench would be sending out the real signals to Giants players.

Even the greatest tacticians cannot succeed without first-rate players, and Foster was able to put together an all-star squad. John Henry Lloyd was lured back to Chicago from New York's Lincoln Giants. Second baseman Elwood "Bingo" DeMoss combined with him to form perhaps the greatest double-play combination in baseball history. Center fielder Oscar Charleston batted, ran, fielded, and some say fought better than anyone else. Pitcher Cannonball Dick Redding's fastball lived up to his nickname.

Foster's Chicago American Giants were not the only great black team of this period. The Lincoln Giants proved nearly invincible in their eastern contests. Pitcher Joe Williams (whose speed earned him the nicknames "Smokey Joe" and "Cyclone Joe") and outfielder Spotswood Poles (called the "black Ty Cobb") led the team. Pitcher Sam Streeter claimed, "It used to take two catchers to hold [Williams]. By the time the fifth inning was over, that catcher's hand would

Smokey Joe Williams

be all swollen. He'd have to have another catcher back there the rest of the game."[4]

A different team dominated baseball on the prairies. In 1912 J. L. Wilkinson, who was white, founded the All Nations team. This team had black, white, Cuban, Japanese, Mexican, Hawaiian, and Native American players, plus a woman known as Carrie Nation (named after the famed antisaloon crusader) at second base. Wrestlers and a band traveled with the club. Small-town residents could enjoy a ball game, wrestling match, and dance in one day.

All Nations was more than a multiethnic entertainment show. The team played superior baseball. Virgil Barnes later pitched with the New York Giants. Mound mates Jose Mendez, John Donaldson, and Bill Drake also would have pitched in the majors if given a chance.

Despite the powers of these teams, Foster's Chicago American Giants were the nation's foremost black team, and their abilities showed at the box office. On one Sunday in 1911, the Chicago Cubs drew 6,000 fans, the White Sox attracted 9,000, and the American Giants pulled in 11,000.

Their reputation became a lure to Chicago for players and fans alike. The *Chicago Defender* reminded readers that the American Giants were the best black team in the country. Foster told young baseball prospects that they could live in chicago, travel by Pullman, and "play with the great Rube Foster."[5]

The main lure of Chicago for most southern blacks was not Rube Foster or baseball, but jobs. During World War I, northern cities had industrial jobs and needed people to fill them. Black southerners flocked to Chicago, Detroit, Cleveland, and other cities in the north to make money and enjoy freedom unimaginable back home. Chicago, for example, gained 200,000 black residents between 1910 and 1920.[6]

Blacks now had numbers in northern cities and enough spending money to support a baseball league. Such a league could improve the fortunes of all member clubs by promoting pennant races. The league also could solve other problems: players who jumped from team to team, undependable team schedules, and overreliance on booking agents who took 10 to 40 percent of the gate.

Foster met with the representatives of other black teams at a Kansas City YMCA on February 13, 1920, and created the Negro National League. Member teams in this new league included the Chicago American Giants, Chicago Giants, St. Louis Giants, Dayton Marcos, Detroit Stars, Indianapolis ABCs, Kansas City Monarchs, and Cuban Stars (who spent their entire first season playing road games but later based themselves in Cincinnati). The league banned raids on one another's teams and instituted fines for ungentlemanly conduct. Negro National League teams played 60 to 80 league games per year. The rest of the time they devoted to 100 or more exhibition games.

All the owners except J. L. Wilkinson, the former All Nations owner who now had the Monarchs franchise, were black. Foster originally opposed Wilkinson, but other black owners liked and respected him. He could keep peace if interracial problems arose. Just as important, he held the lease to the Kansas City ballpark.

Even more than his desire for a united, stable league, Foster had a higher dream. He hoped for acceptance from the white major leagues. Perhaps someday, the Negro National League winner would play the major-league World Series winner in a real championship. Or perhaps the day might arrive when black and white players competed on the same team. Foster wanted black players to maintain a high standard of play, to be ready in case that ever happened.

Unfortunately for Foster, the wait would be a long one, in part because of the 1919 World Series. In that contest the Chicago White Sox lost the Series to Cincinnati, and eight White Sox were accused of throwing the games. Major-league owners, in an attempt to rid the game of corruption, hired a commissioner and gave him absolute powers.

Kenesaw Mountain Landis, a federal judge, was the owners' choice.

Black players had no friend in him. In 1923 Landis prohibited major-league teams from playing black squads in postseason games. "Mr. Foster, when you beat our teams it gives us a black eye," he explained.[7]

Foster exercised more absolute power in his league than Landis did in the majors. He knew the league needed balanced teams to sustain interest in all cities. He helped create that balance by shifting star players to weaker franchises—including moving his best outfielder, Oscar Charleston, to Indianapolis. Foster even dictated the pitching rotations. Top pitchers faced each other on Sundays, when teams drew the biggest crowds.

His maneuverings proved successful. The Negro National League drew 400,000 fans its first season. Total combined salaries of players leaped from $30,000 in 1919 to $75,000 in 1920.

Although no formal standings were announced, the Chicago American Giants claimed the 1920 pennant. Foster's team also won in 1921 and 1922. Word of the league's success reached the East Coast, and owners there decided to form a league to match Foster's midwestern organization.

The Eastern Colored League was organized in 1923. Six teams joined: the Hilldales of suburban Philadelphia; Brooklyn Royal Giants; Bachrach Giants of Atlantic City, New Jersey; Baltimore Black Sox; New York Lincoln Giants; and Havana Cuban Stars of New York. Each owner was a co-commissioner, but the league's real power lay with Nat Strong, the league's booking agent.

Foster and Strong, who had little use for each other, made peace long enough to arrange a world series between their leagues' champions in 1924. The Monarchs represented the NNL against the ECL Hilldales. Nine games were played in Philadelphia, Baltimore, Kansas City, and Chicago. The series was tied after eight games and scoreless going into the eighth inning of the finale. Kansas City then exploded for five runs, and Jose Mendez's two-hit shutout gave the Monarchs victory. The following year the Hilldales, led by third baseman William "Judy" Johnson, took five out of six games from the Monarchs.

Kenesaw Mountain Landis

Negro-league world series were never as profitable as white ones. The 1924 games averaged about 5,000 fans per game. The winning Monarchs made $308. The six games in 1925 attracted about 3,000 fans each. Winning Hilldales received $58 apiece, less than they could have made from a reasonable barnstorming tour.

The American Giants beat the Bachrach Giants in 1926, before enmity between the leagues curtailed the series. The American Giants also won the 1927 NNL title and black world series, but the team owner's illness made that year's championship a hollow victory.

Foster met with New York Giants manager John McGraw and American League president Ban Johnson in 1926, hoping to arrange games between the American Giants and major-league teams. No one ever discussed the outcome of the talks, but obviously they were not successful.

Afterward, Foster's behavior changed radically. He began chasing phantom fly balls in front of his home. Without warning, he would break into a full run. He locked himself in his bathroom and refused to leave. He told his wife he was needed to pitch in the World Series. Rube Foster, a genius as a player, manager, and executive, had suffered a nervous breakdown.

He was sent to a mental hospital in Kankakee, Illinois, where he spent the remaining four years of his life. In December 1930, 3,000 people attended his funeral. The Negro National League sent a 200-pound floral baseball of white chrysanthemums, with red roses for the seams. The *Defender* claimed he "had died a martyr to the game, the most commanding figure baseball had ever known."[8]

Chapter 4

LIFE ON THE ROAD— "YOU GOT USED TO IT"

White boys in the early years of the century dreamed of becoming major-league baseball players. Not only could they play the game they loved, but they could live like kings. The best hotels, the fanciest restaurants, and the finest train cars awaited major leaguers.

Black boys could also dream of becoming professional baseball players and playing the game they loved. But those who made it in black baseball hardly led the life of royalty. Instead Negro-league baseball usually offered long and tiring rides, second-rate sleeping accommodations, and exhausting games. If players got a day off, it was thanks to a rain cloud and not the schedule maker.

Negro leaguers, like major leaguers, went south early each spring. Major leaguers spent the first weeks of their spring training loosening up in Florida, Arizona, or California. Negro leaguers went straight to work. Roy Campanella, who starred first with the Baltimore Elite Giants and later with the Brooklyn Dodgers, recalled:

> In the big leagues, the first week and more is spent pretty much just loosening the winter kinks and getting your arms and legs in shape. But that's not how it was—ever—in the Negro leagues. No sooner did you pull on your uniform than you were in a game, playing before paying customers. . . . Man, we didn't just sop up sun and orange

juice. . . . No sir—[we had] regular exhibition games with the hat being passed.[1]

Opponents at these games could be anybody—another Negro-league team, a black semipro squad, a factory team, or a railroad team, for example. Black colleges such as Fisk and Morehead fielded strong clubs. The Southern Negro League, formed shortly after the NNL, usually provided a stiff challenge.

Where white leagues spent much of spring training on instruction, black leagues had no such luxury. "We just didn't have the time to teach anybody anything," Buck Leonard recalled.[2]

Southern jaunts also served as scouting expeditions for promising players. Even Southern Negro League teams were fair game. Since many southern states did not allow black teams to play white ones, there was the possibility for SNL players to play more games—and make more money—in the North. Scouting was haphazard. Buck Leonard, the "black Lou Gehrig," languished 12 years in rural North Carolina before a Negro-league team noticed him.

By the middle of April, the 14-player teams were ready to move north. They played their way home, finding games all along the route. By the end of April, it was time for their home opening day.

Opening day was an unofficial holiday in Negro-league cities. Black entertainers and politicians (plus white politicians who courted black votes) were ready to toss the first pitch. The Kansas City Monarchs started their season with a parade to the park that attracted bands and thousands of followers.[3] Newark Eagles owner Effa Manley remembered, "Oh, boy, did they dress. People came out who didn't know the ball from the bat. All the girls got new outfits."[4]

League games were usually reserved for Saturdays and Sundays, when workers and their families were free to come to the park. Between those weekends, a team might find a dozen other games in four or five states.

A packed stadium on opening day of a Negro-league season

"I sure get a laugh when I see in the papers where some major league pitcher says he gets a sore arm because he's overworked and he pitches every four days," said pitching great Leroy "Satchel" Paige. "Man, that'd be just a vacation for me."[5]

Days off did not exist for Negro-league players. "You were always booked to play somewhere every day," recalled Buck Leonard. "There never came a day we weren't booked to play somewhere. Never."[6]

Usually, it was several games. Third baseman Judy Johnson remembered, "We'd play three games at a time, a doubleheader and a night game, and you'd get back to the hotel and you were tired as a yard dog."[7]

From April until October, major leaguers played only against one another. But a Negro-league team might play another league team, a talented semipro squad, an improvised small-town team, or, after the World Series, an "all-star" team featuring one or more major leaguers.

They played in big and small cities. But their most receptive audiences were in small towns. In the days before television, when few towns had a movie theater and few residents had a car, the visit from a traveling baseball team was a major highlight of the year. Black and white fans alike would flock to the ballfield in hopes of seeing the local high-school star get a hit off Wilbur "Bullet Joe" Rogan or strike out Norman "Turkey" Stearnes. The small-town teams usually had to guarantee the black team a fee—$500 or 60 percent of the proceeds.

Players sometimes hid their real skills during these games. There was nothing to be gained by trouncing such an opponent, and they wanted to be invited back next year. A young player might gain some experience, or a veteran might try his hand at a different position. And small-town games were not always easy. Monarchs first baseman John "Buck" O'Neil recalled, "We were more than this team traveling around. We were the guys everybody wanted to beat. There were no routine or easy games. We're the game of a lifetime for a lot of these semipro teams, the game of a lifetime, and they played their heart out against us."[8]

After the game, the town might have a picnic, and ballplayers would share in the fried chicken, bread, salad, and pies prepared for the occasion. Most likely, however, they were already in their bus or car, making a several hours' trip to their next game.

Whatever it took, black ballplayers made it from one game to the next. Top clubs like the Kansas City Monarchs or Chicago American Giants rode first-class, in private Pullman train cars, during the 1920s. Later, when the Depression hit the United States in the 1930s, teams scheduled more games in smaller towns. That meant abandoning the trains and riding buses or cars to towns off the rail lines.

"Riding the bus was like having the flu," said Elite Giants pitcher Joe

36   ★ THE NEGRO BASEBALL LEAGUES ★

Black. "You sure didn't like it, but after a few days you got used to it."[9] Players like American Giants third baseman Dave Malarcher, who had been used to Pullman cars, quit rather than accept the buses. But most tolerated the rides. The Homestead Grays averaged about 30,000 miles (48,300 kilometers) a year by bus.

Automobile travel could be unpredictable. Pittsburgh Crawfords outfielder Ted Page described one adventure:

> We were coming through the Catskill Mountains . . . and we had two Pierce Arrow cars that we rode in. We had a flat tire in one. I don't know why we didn't have a spare. . . . Anyhow we had to take the other car and go find a tire. Something like one o'clock in the morning coming down the Rip Van Winkle Trail. We finally did go maybe fifteen or twenty miles, found a place open, and bought a tire. Dick [Redding] was the manager, road secretary and everything. So he set the tire on the running board outside, with his hand on it to hold it. I guess everybody fell asleep; I did. And when we got back and stopped, the driver got out and said, "Okay, Dick, come on, give me the tire." Dick says, "Huh? What?" He jumped up, got outside the car, there was no tire there! We had gone to sleep, and the tire had rolled away someplace. We had to go back and buy another tire, because Dick went to sleep.[10]

If the vehicle was uncomfortable and sleep was out of the question, players often sang gospel songs. Always, they discussed the previous game. Page said, "When we lost a game, we'd sit up practically all night discussing it. Why did we do that? This is the way I had to keep from washing windows in a downtown store or sweeping a floor."[11]

Transportation was only part of black ballplayers' hardships. Once they

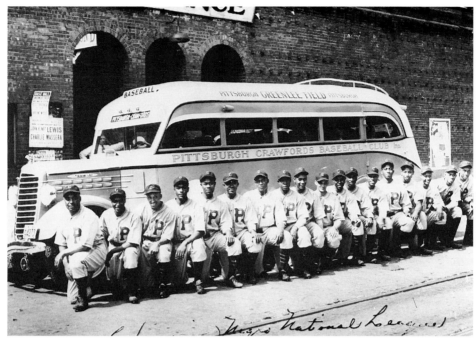

The Pittsburgh Crawfords and the tour bus they traveled in around the country

reached their destination, particularly in the South, finding a place to sleep or a bite to eat often presented a challenge.

Even in the North, white hotel owners often did not allow blacks to stay in their hotels. In the South, integrated sleeping facilities were virtually nonexistent. Black players might find an all-black hotel. If not, there might be a rooming house, a fan's home, or a black church.

When they could find a hotel, it was often less than top quality. Leonard recalled, "Sometimes we'd stay in hotels that had so many bedbugs you had to put a newspaper down between the mattress and the sheets."[12]

Sometimes, particularly if riding all night, they did not find a place to sleep. When they got to the ballpark, three or four players would sleep through the first game of a doubleheader. These refreshed players would take the field in the second game and allow some teammates to rest. Occasionally a manager would have to run to a team bus or car to awaken a sleeping relief pitcher.[13]

Often, a meal was as hard to find as a bed. Jack Marshall, an infielder with the Chicago American Giants, remembered:

> When we left Chicago to go to St. Louis and play, there was no place between here and St. Louis where we could stop and eat—not unless we stopped in a place where they had a colored settlement. From St. Louis to Kansas City, same thing. So many times we would ride all night and not have anything to eat, because they wouldn't feed you.
>
> Going from Chicago to Cleveland, same thing. So the boys used to take sardines and a can of beans and pour them into one of those bell jars. They'd take some crackers, too, and that was their food—they'd eat out of that bell jar. That's the way they had to do it.[14]

Conditions in the South ranged from highly uncomfortable to terrifying. Everything—restaurants, hotels, even rest rooms and drinking fountains—was segregated. Black newspapers were filled with stories of lynchings—killings of blacks by whites. The Ku Klux Klan held open rallies that served to frighten blacks.

Ted "Double Duty" Radcliffe recalled one weekend in Georgia:

> It was about eight at night. We were ready to go out and do the town, and I mean *do* the town. We had money, we knew where the nightclubs were. We were ready to party.
>
> But as they were about to leave, news arrived that a black driver had hit a white child and cops were willing to grab any blacks on the street to pay for it.
>
> Now we really wanted to go out. We looked at each

other, remembered we were in Georgia, and we took our jackets off. We stayed all night. We weren't taking any chances down there.[15]

Bigotry was not limited to the states of the old Confederacy. Radcliffe recalled, "No place was worse than southern Illinois or Indiana. We once got off the bus to get a drink of water. They said, 'Get off that hose . . . and drink a Coca-Cola. White folks drink from the hose.'"[16]

Whether teams were at home or on the road, game conditions were often less than ideal. The quality of umpiring was uneven at best. Catcher Lloyd "Pepper" Bassett said, "There was no umpiring, only guesses."[17] The home team supplied the umps, who were more likely to call in favor of neighbors than strangers. Ironically, bad umpires might have helped Negro-league players, by forcing them to hit any pitches in or near the strike zone.

Baseballs stayed in games until the stuffing was literally knocked out of them. Batters had to face balls that were nicked, scratched, battered, and bruised. The spitball, shine ball, emery ball—pitches long outlawed in the majors—were still common. Any pitch could have the wild gyrations of a knuckleball. Occasionally the teams lost even these browned-up balls. Outfielder Charlie Biot recalled, "I remember my team, the Baltimore Elite Giants, played the Homestead Grays in Richmond, and at the end of the seventh inning they just plumb ran out of baseballs. No baseballs. They had to find a guy in the stands who owned a sports shop in town to drive down and get us some baseballs."[18]

Records from Negro-league games were sketchy. A player assigned to keep score might not have done it properly or might have been called into the game. Cool Papa Bell said, "I remember one game I got five hits and stole five bases, but none of it was written down because they forgot to bring the scorebook to the game that day."[19]

The hardships they faced led to ingenious solutions. Negro-league pitchers were not afraid to throw the ball at batters' heads. (Buck Leonard commented, "We had to learn to duck as well as hit."[20]) A pitcher once knocked Kansas City Monarchs shortstop Willie Wells cold with a pitch. Soon afterward, Wells passed a construction site before a game. He borrowed a hard hat and became the first player to wear a batting helmet.

Even though living and playing conditions paled in comparison with those of white players, Negro-league ballplayers thrived in comparison with most of black America at the time. Most professions (except for the ministry or teaching) were closed or only partially opened to blacks. With baseball being the only major professional sport, ballplayers enjoyed high status in the black community wherever they played. During the Depression, ballplayers earned $2,000 or $3,000 a year, when a typical black worker might be lucky to get $20 a month.

Most took their position as role models seriously. "You had standards you had to live up to," said second baseman Sammy T. Hughes.[21] Country-born players with coarse ways were given new suits. More educated players helped them adapt to city life. Ballplayers as well as management on the Kansas City Monarchs picked players they thought were good enough morally as well as physically to play on the team.[22]

They mingled with fans in a manner more intimate than that of most major leaguers. A youngster named Henry Wiggins brought his mitt to a game, and Philadelphia's star third baseman Judy Johnson spotted him. Wiggins recalled, "The great Judy Johnson said, 'Kid, come on, let's take your glove off, play catch.' One of the greatest thrills of my life! I told my dad I played catch with Judy Johnson!"[23]

Although players occasionally suffered from the often rough life, few regretted it. Buck O'Neil commented, "Don't feel sorry for me. I had a beautiful life. I played with the greatest ballplayers in the world, and I played against the best ballplayers in the world. I saw this country and a lot of other countries, and I met some wonderful people."[24]

Chapter 5

SATCH

Thousands of players roamed North America with Negro-league teams during the segregation era, but one was more famous than the rest put together. A lanky pitcher named Leroy Robert "Satchel" Paige gained renown among black and white fans alike. No pitcher matched his speed and control. And no pitcher—or any other player in all of baseball—matched his showmanship.

Where did Satchel Paige pitch? Where *didn't* he pitch? He was a walking geography lesson. Homestead, Pennsylvania; Gulfport, Mississippi; Chattanooga, Tennessee; New Orleans; Pittsburgh; Cleveland; Kansas City, Missouri; Baltimore; New York City; Philadelphia; St. Louis; Miami; Portland, Oregon; Bismarck, North Dakota; Pensacola, Florida; Ciudad Trujillo, Dominican Republic; Nashville; Birmingham—these cities were only a few whose names appeared on the estimated 250 uniforms Paige wore during his professional career. He even donned a false beard and pitched with the traveling religious House of David team.

As with many other legends, details were uncertain about Paige. He said he was born in 1906, although Cleveland Indians owner Bill Veeck once hired a detective who said Paige could not have been born after 1899.[1] As a child, he carried baggage at a train station in Mobile, Alabama. The ingenious youth rigged up a broomstick and tied ropes to it so he could tote more satchels—bags. His job led to his nickname—"Satchel."

A youthful shoplifting conviction that landed him in reform school for five years might have been a blessing in disguise. It kept him out of trouble and gave him a chance to concentrate on baseball.

The Chattanooga Black Lookouts gave him his start in 1926, and soon he joined the top black teams. By the early 1930s he was starring with the Homestead Grays and Pittsburgh Crawfords, two of the greatest Negro-league teams of all time.

Paige developed an array of colorful pitches. There was the "two-hump blooper," a strangely moving change-up. "Little Tom" was his medium fastball, unhittable by most mortals. "Long Tom" was a fastball unhittable by anyone. Later he developed the "hesitation pitch," in which he momentarily stopped before continuing his delivery.

Satchel Paige in his Monarchs uniform

His fastball astounded opposing hitters. Pitcher William "Sug" Cornelius remembered, "Satchel was something to behold. [He'd] show you fast balls here at your knee all day. They looked like a white dot on a sunshiny day—a white dot."[2] Dizzy Dean, the St. Louis Cardinals ace who often opposed him in barnstorming tours, added, "My fastball looked like a change of pace alongside that pistol bullet old Satch shoots up to the plate."[3] Dean once commented, "If Satch and I were pitching on the same team, we'd clinch the pennant by July 4 and go fishing until World Series time."[4]

Along with that speed came near-perfect control. Outfielder Monte Irvin claimed, "He used to warm up by throwing pitches at sixty feet over a dime. Not a plate, but over a dime! And he'd hit the corners on the dime."[5]

Even though he was the highest-salaried player in the Negro leagues, Paige made much more money selling his services independently on a game-by-game basis. He commanded 10 to 15 percent of the gate at any nonleague game where he appeared. At one time he boasted the major leagues could not afford him, and he was probably right. He earned about $40,000 per year, much more than the salary of the average major leaguer.[6] He traveled first-class. While other black players rode jalopies or rattling buses, he took the finest cars or private airplanes. He flaunted Jim Crow laws by refusing to play anywhere he could not get a restaurant meal or hotel room.

Other players sometimes resented the money and attention he received, but they knew that money for him meant money for them also, because his name on a billboard could mean 5,000 to 10,000 extra tickets sold. Monarchs outfielder Othello Renfroe commented, "There's not a Negro baseball player will say anything against Satchel, because he kept our league going. Anytime a team got in trouble, it sent for Satchel to pitch. So you're talking about your bread and butter when you're talking about Satchel."[7]

Although Paige once said, "The best way to approach work is to avoid it at all times,"[8] he seldom lived up to that advice. He pitched in an estimated 2,500 ball games, winning about 2,000 of them—including about 100 no-hitters.[9] These numbers dwarf Cy Young's major-league record of 511 wins and Nolan Ryan's seven no-hitters. "There never was a man on earth who pitched as much as me. But the more I pitched the stronger my arm would get," Paige said.[10]

His single-game performances seemed even more incredible than his overall totals. Once he pitched a perfect game for eight innings and walked the first three batters in the ninth. Signaling all seven fielders to sit down, he then struck out the side on nine pitches.[11]

Another time he walked the bases loaded in a close game in order to face his friend and slugging counterpart, catcher Josh Gibson. When they were teammates and stars, Satch had told Josh, "Some day we're gonna meet up. You're the greatest hitter in Negro baseball, and I'm the greatest pitcher, and we're gonna see who's best." On July 21, 1942, the confrontation took place. Paige yelled to Gibson, "Hey, Josh, you remember the time when I told you about this. Now is the time." Three times he told the slugger to expect a fastball, and each time Gibson swung and missed.[12]

Paige's pitching adventures took him beyond the U.S. border. Baseball fever swept the Dominican Republic in the 1930s. Dominican strongman Rafael Trujillo, up for reelection, wanted to sponsor a championship team to increase his popularity. Trujillo's representatives persuaded Paige to join the president's team for the country's championship series. Paige rounded up several of his Pittsburgh Crawfords teammates, and southward they went. Trujillo treated the ballclub like a national treasure. Their Dominican quarters were constantly under guard, and army troops escorted them to the stadium.

Paige's Ciudad Trujillo team lost the first three games of the crucial series with Trujillo's main foe. They returned to the hotel to find armed militiamen waiting for them. "El Presidente doesn't lose," one of them warned, firing a shot into the air. "You know you are playing for El Presidente."[13] If they had lost, Paige conceded, "We would have passed over the river Jordan."[14] But they won the series, pocketed their $30,000, and returned home as quickly as possible.

A sore arm incurred in 1938 nearly cost Paige his career. He went to

Kansas City Monarchs owner J. L. Wilkinson, who put him on the Monarchs' "B" team. One day, the soreness miraculously disappeared. His arm, now fully restored, led the Monarchs to several titles in following seasons.

It also led him to victories against teams headed by major-league stars like Dizzy Dean and Bob Feller, the Cleveland Indians ace hurler. Feller recalled, "I barnstormed with Satchel Paige annually starting back in 1937 when both of us could really hurl that ball. . . . I had an all-star major league club behind me. They all bore down to see what they could do against a fabled figure such as Paige. They didn't do much."[15]

Years later, Satchel Paige was asked the secret of his success. He gave six rules:

1. Avoid fried meats, which angry up the blood.
2. If your stomach disputes you, lie down and pacify it with cool thoughts.
3. Keep the juices flowing by jangling gently as you move.
4. Go very lightly on the vices, such as carrying on in society—the society ramble ain't restful.
5. Avoid running at all times.
6. And don't look back. Something may be gaining on you.[16]

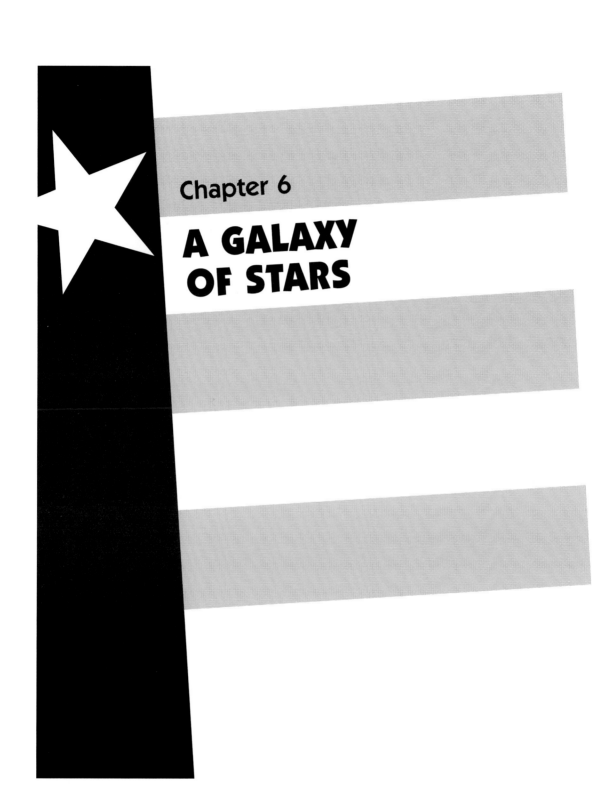

Chapter 6

A GALAXY OF STARS

 atchel Paige was not the only great Negro-league star. Throughout the leagues, diamonds shone with the exploits of outstanding players.

Oscar Charleston

For years major-league baseball fans discussing all-time all-star teams agreed on the same outfield trio. There was hitting and base stealing champ Ty Cobb, powerful slugger Babe Ruth, and offensive and defensive wizard Tris Speaker. Negro-league star Oscar Charleston combined the qualities of all three major-league superstars.

Like Cobb, he was a top hitter and aggressive base runner. Available statistics give him a .353 lifetime batting average. And like the Tigers outfielder, Charleston never ran from a fight. "Charleston would look for them," outfielder Ted Page recalled. "Charleston wasn't temperamental. He was *mean*."[1]

Oscar Charleston

His fearlessness showed itself on a train trip through Florida. James "Cool Papa" Bell related the time that a hooded Ku Klux Klan member walked into Charleston's car and "evidently got pretty mouthy." Charleston pulled off the man's hood, a daring act for a black man in the South. The Klansman returned to his car without a fight.[2]

Like Babe Ruth, Charleston could poke the ball out of the park. During one encounter with Washington Senators ace Walter Johnson, Charleston shouted, "Mr. Johnson, I've heard a lot about your fast ball, and I'm gonna hit it out of here." Charleston struck out twice but also hit a home run to secure a 1–0 victory.[3] He was as popular among black kids as Ruth was among white ones.

Charleston, like Speaker, played a shallow centerfield and covered a huge amount of ground. Page claimed, "He used to play right in back of second base. He would outrun the ball."[4] The acrobatic star even added an extra touch to outfield play. On high fly balls, he sometimes charged in, did a flying forward flip, and landed on his feet to make the catch.[5]

"I could outrun Charleston a bit and maybe others might do this or that better than him," commented Bell. "But putting it all together—the ability to hit, run, field, throw, and hit with power—he was the best I ever saw."[6]

Cool Papa Bell

Satchel Paige liked to tell stories about his sometimes teammate James "Cool Papa" Bell. "One day, when I was pitching to 'Cool,'" Paige said, "he drilled one right through my legs and was hit in the back by his own ground ball when he slid into second."[7] Satch was exaggerating, but not by much.

Bell reportedly could circle the bases in 12 seconds. Olympic sprinting champion Jesse Owens often toured with Negro-league teams and gave running exhibitions, but when challenged by Bell, he said, "I don't want to run today. I didn't bring my track shoes."[8]

Cool Papa Bell

Centerfielder Bell also knew how to field and hit. His batting average regularly topped .400, and he deliberately lost at least one batting title. Near the end of his career, he had a higher batting average than young star Monte Irvin and needed to play the season's last game to qualify for the championship. He sat out the game so that Irvin could get the title and publicity that might help him get to the major leagues. "We wanted to give Irvin a chance to go to the majors," Bell explained later. "We would rather pass something on to the future of the black man."[9]

He began his playing career at age 15 in 1918 and excelled with the St. Louis Stars, Homestead Grays, and Pittsburgh Crawfords. Even as a teenager, he showed poise. "The players said I looked cool out there, so they called me 'Cool.' The manager, Bob Gatewood, said that was not enough and added 'Papa.' That's how I became 'Cool Papa.'"[10]

Longtime friend Satchel Paige called him out of retirement (at age 45) for a barnstorming tour. With Bell on first, Paige sacrificed toward third base. With both pitcher and third baseman going for the ball, Bell streaked around second and headed for the "hot corner." Catcher Ray Partee started running to cover third. Bell passed him and scored.[11]

Judy Johnson

They have called him the "black Pie Traynor," after the acrobatic Pittsburgh Pirates third baseman. But many who saw both said Traynor should have been called the "white Judy Johnson."

Judy Johnson

William Julius Johnson, who got his nickname from an earlier ballplayer named "Judy" Gans, was one of the smartest players in the game. As often as not, he found himself on championship teams like the Hilldales, Grays, and Crawfords.

He was a feared hitter, batting .401 in 1929. But he is best remembered for his fielding artistry and baseball tricks. While a Hilldales pitcher would motion outfielders this way or that, Johnson would be at third base, rubbing the ball with sandpaper. The roughed-up ball enabled the pitcher to throw trick pitches that baffled hitters.

"Judy was the smartest third baseman I ever came across," commented Crawfords teammate Ted Page. "A scientific ballplayer, [he] did everything with grace and poise." Another Crawford, Jimmy Crutchfield, added that he "had a great brain, could anticipate the play, knew what his opponents were going to do."[12]

Martin DiHigo

Who was the most versatile player in baseball history? Many Negro-league fans say it was Martin DiHigo, the Cuban-born star who excelled at all nine positions.

In all baseball history, only Babe Ruth and black star Bullet Joe Rogan combined pitching and hitting as effectively as DiHigo. He once hit a home run an estimated 500 feet (152 meters). He led his league in both batting and home runs in a season. In the 1930s he concentrated more on pitching. He went to Mexico in 1938, threw the first no-hitter in Mexican league history, and led the league with a 0.90 earned run average and .387 batting average. He started his career as a second baseman, later became an outfielder, and occasionally played all nine positions in one game.

Martin DiHigo

DiHigo excelled in thinking as well as in hitting, fielding, running, and pitching. Once, on third base, he yelled, "You balked!" to the opposing pitcher. While the opposing hurler stood and held on to the ball, DiHigo walked all the way to home plate, loudly complaining, touched home, and trotted to the dugout before anyone thought to tag him.[13]

"He was the greatest all-around player I know. He was the best player of all time, black or white. He could do it all," said first base star Buck Leonard. "You take your Ruths, Cobbs, or DiMaggios. Give me DiHigo. Bet I'd beat you almost every time."[14] DiHigo, known as "El Maestro" in Mexico and "El Inmortal" in Cuba, is the only player enshrined in the American, Cuban, Mexican, and Venezuelan baseball halls of fame.

Buck Leonard

The near-unanimous choice for greatest first baseman in Negro-league history is Walter "Buck" Leonard, the "black Lou Gehrig." Leonard had a lot in common with the New York Yankees star. Both were quiet men who played in the shadow of more flamboyant teammates. While Gehrig accompanied Babe Ruth in the Yankee lineup, lefty Leonard played with Josh Gibson, the "black Babe Ruth."

A smooth-fielding first sacker often compared to St. Louis Browns great George Sisler, Leonard matched Sisler and Gehrig as a hitter. His lifetime batting average for league games where records exist was .342.

Unlike most Negro-league players, who jumped from team to team, Buck Leonard stayed with the Homestead Grays for 17 seasons, from 1934 until 1950. During that time, from 1937 to 1945, he led the Grays to 9 consecutive Negro National League championships.

Buck Leonard

Josh Gibson

You can take Babe Ruth or Hank Aaron, Jimmie Foxx or Willie Mays. Those who saw Josh Gibson called him the greatest slugger the game has ever known. His statistics—nine home run and four batting titles in 13 Negro-league seasons and a .384 lifetime batting average, the highest in Negro-league history—do not begin to describe his overwhelming presence.

Gibson once clouted the ball so far in Monessen, Pennsylvania, that the mayor stopped the game to measure the ball's 512-foot (156-meter) journey. He once hit an upper-deck home run with one hand. During one season with the Homestead Grays, he hit more home runs into Washington's Griffith Stadium than all of the American League players (except for the Senators) combined. He sometimes guaranteed to hit two home runs in a game, and he once hit 85 home runs in a season.

His 1930 entry into the Negro leagues was the stuff of dreams. The Homestead Grays' regular catcher Buck Ewing broke his finger during a game. Grays manager Judy Johnson asked Gibson, a well-known Pittsburgh semipro catcher who was sitting in the stands, to replace Ewing.

Josh Gibson

Some called him a very good catcher; others said he was only average. But nobody ever doubted his hitting, although some might have questioned some of the stories told about his power. According to one tale, he once hit the ball so high and far in Pittsburgh that no one saw it come down. Gibson's Crawfords were playing the next day in Philadelphia when suddenly a ball plummeted from the sky and into the glove of an amazed center fielder. The umpire pointed to Gibson and shouted, "Yer out—yesterday in Pittsburgh!"[15]

Chapter 7

MONARCHS, GRAYS, AND CRAWFORDS

The illness and death of Rube Foster nearly meant the end for organized black baseball. The Eastern Colored League had collapsed in 1928. A successor, the American Negro League, lasted only one season. The Negro National League survived Foster, but only by a year. Weak league leadership and economic ruin throughout the country caused by the Great Depression toppled the NNL in 1931. For a year, the feeble Southern Negro League was the only black organized baseball league left.

But black baseball rebounded to survive and even thrive in the 1930s. Three dominant owners led superior teams during this era. They had as little as possible to do with one another but had several points in common: generosity, the admiration of their players, and the ability to put together some of the greatest baseball teams in history.

Rube Foster had hesitated to admit J. L. Wilkinson into his newly created Negro National League. Wilkinson, after all, was a white man, and Foster feared eventual white takeover of a successful black enterprise. Ironically, Wilkinson did the most to sustain black baseball after Foster's passing.

Wilkinson's Kansas City Monarchs left the Negro National League soon after Foster's illness, finding it was more profitable to barnstorm full-time around prairie America. They played against anyone who might draw an audience, including famed female athlete Babe Didrikson and the bearded religious team known as the House of David.

But the economic collapse that put a quarter of the nation out of work had its effect on baseball. Most working people had daytime jobs and could not leave to attend games. Attendance at major-league and Negro-league games suffered.

Wilkinson came up with an innovation that ultimately helped save black baseball—lights and night games. Various people had experimented with baseball under the lights since the 1880s, but Wilkinson was the first to succeed with a lighting system used for most of his team's games. "What talkies are to the movies, lights will be to baseball," he predicted.[1]

Since his was a traveling team, he had to devise a portable system. In late 1929 he spent $50,000 on it. He bought several trucks, each one supporting two poles that each held six floodlights. When the Monarchs got to whatever field they were playing on, derricks raised the 45-foot (14-meter) poles into the air. A 250-horsepower generator provided the power.

On April 28, 1930, Wilkinson brought the Monarchs and lights into Enid, Oklahoma. Three thousand fans braved threatening weather to watch the Monarchs beat the Phillips University team, 12–3. Monarchs pitcher Chet Brewer remembered, "When they turned that on, it was light as day out. Those lights were beautiful. . . . That was the birth of night baseball."[2]

Within weeks, the traveling light system had paid for itself. Where 2,000 or 3,000 fans might have seen Monarchs day games, more than 10,000 came for night contests. The Monarchs and their traveling light show delighted crowds from Denver to Winnipeg to Pittsburgh. The Monarchs and Grays played the first night game in Pittsburgh, the game where a catcher's injury gave Josh Gibson his start in Negro-league baseball.

Wilkinson's lights saved the Monarchs and black baseball, because other teams adopted his innovation. Lights even greatly helped the major leagues. Five years after Wilkinson's game, the Cincinnati Reds hosted major-league baseball's first night game. Within a few years, most big-league teams were playing almost all of their games under the lights.

By the mid-1930s, Wilkinson's teams became as impressive as his lights.

Putting on a Monarchs uniform was as much an honor for black players as a New York Yankees uniform was for white major leaguers. Pitcher Hilton Smith said, "Everybody, *everybody* that played baseball wanted to play with the Monarchs."[3]

The Pittsburgh area boasted two of the greatest black teams. First came the Homestead Grays, based in an industrial suburb of the city. Grays owner Cumberland "Cum" Posey was an outstanding athlete in his own right, at one time considered the top black basketball player in the country. A Penn State alumnus, he was an educated and refined man who served on the local school board.

Posey had taken over the Grays in 1920 and built a team that demolished all opposition. With stars like Judy Johnson, Oscar Charleston, Smokey Joe Williams, and Josh Gibson, they finished 143–10 in 1926 and 136–17 in 1931. But Posey faced a problem common to many owners of black teams in the 1930s—he was nearly always broke. This was not a problem shared by his Pittsburgh counterpart, W. A. "Gus" Greenlee.

Wilkinson and Posey were solid, upright citizens. Greenlee made his money through the numbers game, a form of lottery popular mainly in the black community. Today lotteries are legal in most states. In the 1930s the numbers game was illegal and Greenlee was often afoul of the law.

Whether it was legally earned or not, Greenlee had lots of money in a time when high-paying legal jobs were closed to most blacks. Author Richard Wright noted that there was no stigma to the numbers bosses then, commenting, "They would have been steel tycoons, Wall Street brokers, or auto moguls had they been white."[4] Furthermore, Greenlee enjoyed a reputation for "honesty." Unlike some of his competitors, Greenlee always paid off all wins in full.

Greenlee invested part of his numbers money in the Crawford Grille, a restaurant and dance hall in the black Hill section of Pittsburgh. The large, nattily dressed man also began a team called the Crawford Colored Giants (later shortened to Crawfords) in 1930.

When Posey's bankroll started to fail him in 1932, Greenlee hired away the crosstown baseball stars. When he purchased two seven-passenger Lincoln luxury cars, Homestead Grays players Satchel Paige and Josh Gibson joined him. Greenlee also snatched Oscar Charleston, Ted Page, Ted "Double Duty" Radcliffe (who earned his nickname by catching the opening game of a doubleheader and pitching a shutout in the nightcap), Johnny Russell, Jake Stephens, Jud Wilson, and Judy Johnson from the Grays. Outfielders Jimmy Crutchfield, Rap Dixon, Sam Bankhead, and Cool Papa Bell were lured from other clubs. Charleston, then a first baseman, managed the Crawfords, perhaps the greatest baseball team ever to don a uniform.

This first-class club got a first-class stadium in 1933. Greenlee spent $100,000 to build 5,000-seat Greenlee Field, the first professional ballpark owned by blacks and also the first professional park with permanent lights.

Greenlee also organized a new Negro National League in 1933. Member teams the first year included the Crawfords, Grays, Chicago American Giants, Baltimore Black Sox, Nashville Elite Giants, Detroit Stars, and Columbus Blue Birds. Greenlee's rival, the Grays, joined the first year but soon were kicked out for attempting to raid players from other clubs (the kind of action Greenlee and the Crawfords had taken on the Grays). They returned to the league two years later.

For the most part these teams were run by gangsters, who, after all, were the only blacks who could spend sufficient money on a ballclub. Greenlee, who ran one of the most successful teams, admitted that he had lost $30,000 on his team in 1932 alone.[5] Greenlee never worried about the baseball losses. The team helped publicize his restaurant and other profit-making businesses. Also, Greenlee and other owners used their baseball teams as a financial front to cover up some of their less-than-legal activities.

Four years later southern and midwestern clubs—the Detroit Stars, American Giants, Kansas City Monarchs, Memphis Red Sox, Birmingham Black Barons, Indianapolis Athletics, and St. Louis Stars—formed the

Negro American League, a league less dependent on gangster capital.[6]

Like Wilkinson and Posey, Greenlee was generous to his players. One winter, Ted Page found himself without a job. Greenlee hired him as a numbers lookout. Page's only task was to ring a bell if a police officer or other suspicious person approached Greenlee's gambling headquarters.[7]

As might be expected from someone of his "profession," Greenlee often found ways to skirt the rules. Pennsylvania state law prohibited professional baseball games on Sundays. Greenlee got around it by scheduling a ball game for 12:01 A.M. Monday.

Greenlee ran into other occupational problems in 1937. His political friends, who offered him protection, lost elections. Players saw his problems and were ready to jump the team at the first good offer. When dictator Rafael Trujillo offered Satchel Paige and other stars high salaries to play in the Dominican Republic, most jumped the team. Most former Crawfords did not return to Pittsburgh when the Dominican tournament ended. After 1938 the Pittsburgh Crawfords were no more.

Posey, meanwhile, rebuilt the Grays into a championship squad. In 1934 he signed William "Buck" Leonard, the slugger who became the greatest first baseman in Negro-league history. A year later he took a partner, Rufus "Sonnyland" Jackson, who had an ample bankroll to sign other stars. The Grays moved their weekend home games to large stadiums—Saturday home games in the Pittsburgh Pirates' Forbes Field and Sunday home games in Washington, D.C. (where they outdrew bland Senators teams).

When the Dominican tournament ended, Josh Gibson came to Pittsburgh, but not to play with the Crawfords. He joined Leonard on the Grays, forming a home run combination rivaled in baseball history only by the New York Yankees' Babe Ruth and Lou Gehrig. The Grays won Negro National League championships nine consecutive years (1937 to 1945), a record for professional teams. After the black world series was reintroduced in 1942, the Grays played in four of them, winning in 1943 and 1944.

Chapter 8

"THEY CONSIDERED US EQUALS"

Without a doubt, the games Negro-league teams relished most were those against teams with major-league players. If black players could not play on major-league teams, they could show they were the equals of major-league players by downing them in exhibition games.

Beat them they did. From 1900 until 1950, black teams won 268 recorded games against teams with major-league players. The white teams won only 168 games.[1]

"So far as the competition, I could see no difference in the major leagues and our own leagues, as far as hitting against the different pitchers," recalled Gene Benson, an outfielder with the Philadelphia Stars. "When we played head to head, it was nip and tuck. They won some and we won some. The white ballplayers knew it. They respected us. They considered us equals."[2]

Ever since Andrew Foster had earned the nickname "Rube" by defeating Philadelphia Athletics ace Rube Waddell in 1902, black victories over white stars were legendary. Cuban hurler Jose Mendez made himself a Caribbean hero in 1908 by blanking the visiting Cincinnati Reds on one hit. Fireballing pitcher Smokey Joe Williams shut out both the New York Giants and New York Yankees within two weeks in 1912. He beat the National League champion Philadelphia Phillies 1–0 after the 1915 season.

Judge Kenesaw Mountain Landis was appointed baseball commissioner in 1920. In three years, he outlawed exhibition games between major-league teams and Negro-league squads. Players skirted this ban by forming "all-star" teams. These consisted of stars from various major-league teams, or a major leaguer or two plus several minor leaguers.

Even minor-league teams apparently were not immune from the ban. The Kansas City Blues, a white team, faced off against the Monarchs in the early 1920s. When the Monarchs won five out of six games in 1922, the Blues called off the series, perhaps on orders from the commissioner.

With or without Landis's approval, games between black teams and white stars continued. Contests between Satchel Paige and Dizzy Dean or Bob Feller drew 30,000 fans, no matter where they played. Despite the intense rivalries, white and black players alike thoroughly enjoyed the competition. "Bob Feller and Dizzy Dean were some of the greatest friends I had in baseball," Pittsburgh Crawfords star Ted Radcliffe said.[3]

Granted, blacks enjoyed an advantage in these games. Pitcher Bill Foster explained, "We were organized as a unit, but they just came down there with one from here, one from there. They didn't have a whole lot of signals or anything like that. In other words, an all-star, picked ball club is at a disadvantage."[4]

Almost without exception, the top Negro-league stars hammered the major-league players. Smokey Joe Williams posted a 19–7 record against major leaguers (including eight wins and a tie against future Hall of Famers). Webster McDonald was 14–4 against major-league all-star teams. Jose Mendez won 25 of 38 games. Dave Malarcher hit .368; Josh Gibson, .424; Cool Papa Bell, .405; Rap Dixon, .372; George "Mule" Suttles, .374, with 11 homers in 23 games; Ted Page, .429; Willie Wells, .392. Spotswood Poles, the "black Ty Cobb," lived up to his nickname with a .610 batting average against major-league players and teams.

Still, players and fans of all races after 1923 missed the best possible matchups—the top black versus the top white teams. Morris Wilentsky, a fan of both black and white baseball games, commented, "I saw 'em all, every team there was, and I'm telling you, if they could have put the Pittsburgh Crawfords of 1936, with Paige and Gibson, up against the Yankees, with DiMaggio, it would have been the greatest series of games of all time, and I couldn't tell you who would have won."[5]

One of the many Latin American teams that offered Negro-league and major league players a chance to play together

Black and white stars also played alongside one another as teammates—but not in the United States. During winters, teams from Latin American countries welcomed the best American baseball stars. These top players were black as often as white, a sign that Latin teams deemed the Negro-league players at least the equals of their white counterparts.

One favorite playing ground was Cuba. Americans occupying Cuba after the Spanish-American War introduced baseball, and Cubans took to it with a frenzy. The American League champion Detroit Tigers, minus several of the team's stars, played teams with Cubans and American blacks in 1909. The Tigers won only 4 of 12 games.

After 1910 the Tigers returned to Cuba. This time they brought outfielder Ty Cobb, the best hitter and base stealer in the game. Cobb's .371 average during the series roughly matched his .367 lifetime batting average. But in games against black players, Cobb met his match. Catcher Bruce Petway hit .390, Home Run Johnson hit .412, and John Henry Lloyd hit a lofty .500. Southerner Cobb, embarrassed at being shown up by black players, vowed never to play against blacks again. He never did.

Ty Cobb was not the only player bested by John Henry Lloyd, who wielded both bat and glove more dangerously than any other black player of the early 1900s. Major leaguers often called him the "black Honus Wagner," comparing him to the famed shortstop. Wagner himself commented, "After I saw him, I felt honored they should name such a player after me."[6]

Latin American players called him "La Cuchara" ("the scoop") for his ability to shovel tough grounders from the dirt. His huge hands allowed him to make bare-handed pickups and rifle hard-hit balls to first base. He got a superb jump on the ball, thanks to his ability to spot the ball's direction by the batter's swing. As a batter, he hit at or near .400 several times.

Lloyd played with several top teams. "Wherever the money is, that's where I am," he explained.[7] His money, nevertheless, fell far short of what his white counterparts received. Lloyd earned about $250 a month in 1915. Tris Speaker, the Red Sox's star outfielder, made $18,500 that year.

Sportswriter Graham McNamee once asked Babe Ruth who was the greatest player of all time.

"You mean in the major leagues?" asked Ruth. "No," replied McNamee. "Ever."

"In that case," Ruth replied, "I'd pick John Henry Lloyd."[8]

The Cincinnati Reds, who had also played games on the island, signed several top Cuban players. Rafael Almeida played three years for Cincinnati, and Armando Marsans played eight years for the Reds and other teams. Pitcher Adolfo Luque won nearly 200 games in the majors, including 27 for the Reds in 1923.

Black players in the United States hoped the Cuban signings might lead to the eventual entry of American-born black players. But Almeida, Marsans, and Luque were all light-skinned players who were accepted as white. Darker-skinned Cubans were treated like the players of the Negro leagues. Jose Mendez, a coal-complexioned pitcher at least the equal of Luque, was barred from the major leagues. So was Cristobal Torriente, a kinky-haired slugger of far greater ability than either Almeida or Marsans.

After the grueling conditions of Negro-league games and barnstorming tours, the seasons in Mexico or Cuba or Puerto Rico or Venezuela might have seemed like a vacation to the black players. They played two or three games a week, not two or three games a day. Fans showed their appreciation for outstanding batting or pitching performances by stuffing bills through fences. Homestead Grays pitcher Wilmer Fields recalled, "You'd hit a game-winning home run and you'd trot back there and collect yourself one or two hundred extra dollars."[9]

These games gave the black players a chance to live and play in a prejudice-free environment, stay in spacious apartments with maid service, and eat in the finest restaurants. Friendship, not skin color, could be the deciding factor in their off-field associations. Newark Eagles pitcher Max Manning commented, "I remember one trip we made from Philadelphia to Havana. We got on the train in Philadelphia, and we had to stay in a colored-only compartment. We couldn't even leave to get some food. When we finally arrived in Cuba, we were treated as heroes."[10]

The best ballplayers were considered national treasures, particularly in Mexico. Negro-league catcher Quincy Trouppe recalled the time during World War II that he and Theolic Smith could not get draft deferments so that they could play in Mexico. He said, "The representative from Mexico told me that they had loaned the U.S. 80,000 workers to fill the manpower shortages caused by the war and all they wanted in return were two ballplayers named Quincy Trouppe and Theolic Smith."[11]

It was no wonder that some top black players, such as third base stand-out Ray Dandridge, stayed in Latin America for years at a time. Others went there and never bothered to return to the United States.

Despite the ongoing segregation in professional baseball, white players, managers, scouts, and sportswriters always praised the talents of black baseball stars. After a while, the comparisons rang with a similar tone. For example:

- Detroit Tigers second baseman Charlie Gehringer, to pitcher Bill Foster: "If I could paint you white I could get $150,000 for you right now."[12]
- Philadelphia Athletics manager Connie Mack, to third baseman Judy Johnson: "If you were a white boy, you could name your own price."[13]
- New York Giants manager John McGraw, on pitcher John Donaldson: "If Donaldson were a white man, or if the unwritten law of baseball didn't bar Negroes from the major leagues, I would give $50,000 for him and think I was getting a bargain."[14]
- Washington Senators pitching immortal Walter Johnson, on catcher Josh Gibson: "There is a catcher that any big league club would like to buy for $200,000. His name is Gibson. He can do everything. He hits the ball a mile, he catches so easily he might as well be in a rocking chair, throws like a bullet. . . . Too bad this Gibson is a colored fellow."[15]

Even with all these testimonials, the major leagues held the official position that black players were not signed because they were less talented than whites. They stood by this reasoning as another excuse to keep blacks out of the big leagues. Cool Papa Bell commented, "They used to say 'If we find a *good* black player, we'll sign him.' They were lying."[16]

Sometimes black ballplayers got tired of the empty compliments. When Chicago White Sox owner Grace Comiskey told American Giants pitcher Sug Cornelius, "Oh, if you were a white boy, what you'd be worth to my club!" he responded, "I'm not white, I'm black." He added, "I don't know whether I'd change to white if I could."[17]

Slowly, baseball's attitude toward integration began to change. The transformation came not from a sense of black and white but from the color green—the color of money.

Chapter 9

THE ROAD TO INTEGRATION

G us Greenlee, although a prominent Negro-league figure for less than a decade, left an important legacy—the East-West all-star game. When Chicago held its Century of Progress fair in 1933, the American and National leagues played an all-star game between their best players at Chicago's Comiskey Park. A month after the majors held their game, the Negro leagues played their own all-star game, the East-West game. For both white and black leagues, the games proved so popular that they were held annually. While the major leagues rotated the games among the big-league parks, the Negro leagues always held their games in centrally located, accessible Comiskey Park.

"It was more than just an athletic contest," said Newark Eagles pitcher Max Manning. "It was good to look up and see 50,000 up there screaming for you. The game made us big time, just like the major leaguers. The crowds were always mixed, with many whites, and it was terrific."[1]

The East-West game was the largest all-black sporting event in the world, a symbol of racial pride and accomplishment. Heavyweight champion boxer Joe Louis, track star Jesse Owens, bandleader Cab Calloway, and other black sports and entertainment heroes always showed up. South Side blues and jazz nightclubs flourished, entertaining the thousands of visitors who planned their vacations around the game. People came from as far as Los Angeles, New Orleans, and New York. The Union Pacific added extra cars on its Chicago-bound trains during the week of the game.

Even those who could not attend the game were caught up in its excitement. Two major black newspapers, the *Pittsburgh Courier* and *Chicago Defender,* conducted the balloting for the game. By 1939 some players were receiving half a million votes.[2]

Ironically, the East-West game, the greatest achievement of the Negro leagues, helped to their downfall. Attendance figures were not lost on major-league owners. They saw dollars, not fans, in the stands. If black fans had the interest and money to see a black all-star game, then they could help fill major-league stadiums (and owners' pocketbooks) if they could ever play in the majors. Satchel Paige commented, "Those fifty thousand black fans. *That's* what put [blacks] in the majors."[3]

The East-West game was not the only sign of black baseball prosperity. Attendance declined throughout the American and National leagues when top players joined the armed forces in World War II. Negro-league baseball thrived, however. Paige explained, "These days, during the war,

The players of the 1938 East-West game

Monte Irvin

Negro baseball was drawing more fans than it ever did. Everybody had money and everybody was looking for entertainment and they found plenty in Negro baseball. Even the white folks were coming out big."[4]

Black ballplayers as well as white ones served in the armed forces. But while white superstars such as Ted Williams, Hank Greenberg, and Bob Feller were in the army or navy, many of the older black stars—including Satchel Paige, Josh Gibson, Buck Leonard, and Cool Papa Bell—kept playing. They were joined by a new generation of younger stars. The Newark Eagles signed a talented trio, outfielders Monte Irvin and Larry Doby and pitcher Don Newcombe. Fifteen-year-old Baltimore Elite Giants catching sensation Roy Campanella was a living example of baseball's caste system. His father was as Italian as Joe DiMaggio's. But since his mother was black, he was considered black and therefore barred from the majors. While Joe DiMaggio made $50,000 and lived in high style with the New York Yankees, Campanella earned a few hundred dollars a month, often played four games a day, and traveled from town to town on rickety buses.

Even before World War II, whites had begun speaking up for baseball integration. In 1935, *Chicago Tribune* columnist Westbrook Pegler decried the "silly unwritten law that bars dark Babe Ruths and Dizzy Deans from the fame and money they deserve."[5] Shirley Povich of the *Washington Post* wrote in 1941, "There's a couple of million dollars worth of baseball talent on the loose, ready for the big leagues, yet unsigned by any major league. . . . One thing that's keeping them out of the big leagues, the pigmentation of their skin. They happen to be colored."[6]

Some white baseball players also spoke out on behalf of their black compatriots. Lou Gehrig, Gabby Hartnett, Pie Traynor, Paul Waner, and Dizzy Dean were among those who gave support to integration of baseball.

One white player unintentionally aroused more sympathy for blacks than anyone else. Yankee outfielder Jake Powell, asked during a 1938 radio interview what he did during the off-season, replied that he worked as a policeman in Dayton, Ohio, and kept in shape by "cracking niggers in the head."[7] The remarks outraged thousands of blacks and whites alike. The Yankees suspended Powell and later sent him to the minors.

Powell's comment, disgusting though it was, represented only the bigotry of a second-string player. More important, if less direct, were the words and actions of major-league baseball's leading powers.

Homestead Grays pitcher Wilmer Fields commented, "Look, it was never the white ballplayers. We beat them, lost to them, played alongside them in the Caribbean. It was never the fans. We'd fill our seats with white fans. It was never the press—columnists supported us. It was always the owners. They just never wanted black ballplayers."[8]

Sometimes an owner would give a hint at signing a black star. Washington Senators owner Clark Griffith once called Grays stars Josh Gibson and Buck Leonard to his office. Leonard recalled:

> He said, "You played a good ballgame today" and so on and so on. "[We] have been talking about getting you fel-

lows on the Senators team." We said, "…we'd be happy to
play in the major leagues and believe we could make the
major leagues." He said, "Well, I just wanted to see how
you fellows felt about it." We said, "Well, if we were given
the chance, we'd play all right, try to make it. And I believe
we could make it." But we never heard from him again.[9]

Officially, league officials denied that any ban on black players existed.
National League president Ford Frick gave preposterous theories on why
integration would not work. He once said major-league baseball had not
employed black players because the public "has not been educated to the
point where they will accept them."[10] Another time he claimed, incorrectly,
"Colored people did not have a chance to play during slavery. It was more
than fifty years after the introduction of baseball before colored people in
the United States had a chance to play it. Consequently, it was another fifty
years before they arrived at the stage where they were important in the
organized baseball picture."[11] Frick's explanation ignored the fact that black
players had been beating whites for years in exhibition games.

The major culprit behind segregation was Kenesaw Mountain Landis.
The commissioner exercised absolute control over the game. Had he
wanted baseball integration, it could have taken place—but he gave no
indication of wanting it.

Brooklyn Dodgers manager Leo Durocher said he would sign up black
baseball players in a minute if the powers that be would let him. Landis
chewed him out for making that statement, and Durocher later denied it.
The commissioner then announced, "There is no rule, nor to my knowl-
edge has there been, formal or informal, no understanding, sub-terranean
or sub-anything, against the hiring of Negroes in the major leagues."[12]

Landis was careful not to leave any written statement against integration, but his actions spoke volumes. Bill Veeck, son of a former Chicago
Cubs president, attempted to buy the Philadelphia Phillies in 1943. He

planned to elevate the perennial cellar-dwellers by hiring Paige, Gibson, Leonard, Willie Wells, Ray Dandridge, and other black stars for the team.

Veeck made the mistake of telling his plan to Landis. The next morning, he discovered that the Phillies had been sold to the National League. Rather than allow an owner who would bring in the cream of black players, Landis arranged the Phillies' sale to William Cox—who less than a year later was tossed out of baseball for betting on games.[13]

Baseball would never integrate as long as Landis remained commissioner, most blacks conceded. His last word on the subject, to *Courier* writer Wendell Smith, was, "There is nothing further to discuss."[14]

When Landis died in late 1944, baseball owners chose former Kentucky governor Albert "Happy" Chandler as the second commissioner. *Courier* sportswriter Ric Roberts immediately went to Chandler. He related, "Chandler came out immediately, shaking our hands and said, 'I'm for the Four Freedoms. If a black . . . can make it on Okinawa and Guadalcanal . . . he can make it in baseball.' And he told us, 'Once I tell you something, brother, I never change. You can count on me.'"[15]

Despite Chandler's encouragement of blacks, many if not most club owners and league officials were no more anxious to integrate the teams than Landis had been. In early 1945 a secret report written by National League president Frick, American League president Will Harridge, and owners Phillip Wrigley, Larry MacPhail, Sam Breadon, and Tom Yawkey urged that blacks be excluded from the major leagues. A year later 15 owners voted against integration. There was only 1 dissenting vote.

As a player with the St. Louis Browns and a manager with the Browns and Cardinals, Branch Rickey was remembered mainly for his refusal to play or manage on Sundays. Soon, however, he would change baseball history. As general manager of the Cardinals, he instituted the farm system. The Cardinals bought or signed agreements with dozens of minor-league clubs to train players for the majors. Critics charged that the farm system helped

Happy Chandler (center)

kill the minor leagues, but it brought the Cardinals a string of pennants. After a dispute with Cardinal ownership, Rickey joined the Dodgers as president and general manager in 1943.

In early 1945 he announced the formation of the United States League, an all-black major league with white owners. Six teams, including the Brooklyn Brown Dodgers, would be members. Rickey sent scouts throughout the country to look over black stars.

Blacks saw this as an attempt by whites to take over a successful black enterprise. The *Defender*'s Frank Young wrote, "We want Negroes in the major leagues if they have to crawl to get there, but we won't have any major league owners running any segregated leagues for us."[16] Booking agents refused to work for the United States League teams, and the league died before playing a single game.

Was a white-run black major league Rickey's real intention? There were several possible explanations, all of which had to do with money. One reason many owners opposed integration, although none would admit it, was that segregation proved profitable for them. The White Sox, Pirates, Senators, and Giants, among others, charged hefty rents to Negro-league teams for use of their stadiums. The Yankees pocketed $100,000 per year from Negro-league games. Only the Dodgers in New York were shut out. Bill Veeck claimed, "Rickey wanted money. The Yankees and Giants split [the Negro-league money] and Rickey wanted a third of it."[17] Perhaps the United States League was Rickey's way of getting the Dodgers some of that money.

Or perhaps Rickey was using the league as an excuse to scout blacks for the Dodgers without drawing attention to a hidden plan for integrating the major leagues. Ultimately black players wearing Brooklyn Dodger uniforms could mean a bonanza of outstanding players for Brooklyn and many extra dollars from black fans coming to Ebbets Field to cheer their heroes.

As it turned out, Rickey did want to integrate the Dodgers. His method was subtle and his pace slow. He was not looking for just any black player to join the Dodgers. Shortly after Chandler's statement, about blacks' making it in the major leagues, a black reporter pressured Rickey into giving aging veterans Terris McDuffie and Dave "Showboat" Thomas a tryout. Rickey watched them for a few minutes but never gave a serious thought to signing either one. Neither was the type of player he was seeking.

Rickey knew that the first black player in the major leagues would face great problems. In addition to the tension that any rookie faces, there would be abuse from white bigots who hoped the black man would fail. These pressures would be too much for almost any youngster. At the same time, he did not want older players who might play only a year or two in the major leagues. Rickey wanted a good ballplayer, but not necessarily the best one. On-field performance was important, but the man's temperament on and off the field was even more so.

Rickey saw or heard about hundreds of players while conducting tryouts for the United States League. One in particular caught his fancy.

Other than the color of his skin, Jack Roosevelt Robinson had little in common with his fellow Negro-league players. Most were southerners. Robinson, while born in Georgia, grew up and played on integrated sports teams in Pasadena, California. He starred in football, track, and basketball as well as baseball at UCLA before entering the army during World War II. Negro-league players, who knew the sometimes fatal consequences of disobedience in the South, seldom openly questioned the status quo. But while others might have kept silent in the face of obvious injustice, Jackie Robinson acted. Robinson faced a court-martial when he refused to move to the back of an army bus. The military court acquitted him, and soon afterward he applied for and received a discharge.

After leaving the army, Robinson approached the Kansas City Monarchs and tried out as a shortstop. Second baseman Newt Allen commented that Robinson "could run, could hit, and most of all he could think" but "couldn't play shortstop."[18] But when the Monarchs' regular shortstop got injured, Robinson took over there.

Rickey called Robinson to Brooklyn for an interview after the 1945 season. It lasted more than three hours. Rickey shouted and screamed at Robinson, insulting him with the type of abuse he might expect from bigoted white fans as a test to determine whether Robinson could withstand the pressure. Rickey expected Robinson to take it without flinching. At one point Robinson said, "Mr. Rickey, do you want a Negro who is afraid to fight back?" Rickey responded, "I want a ballplayer with guts enough *not* to fight back. You've got to do this job with base hits and stolen bases and fielding ground balls, Jackie. *Nothing* else."[19]

Was Jackie Robinson the best person Rickey could have chosen to break

Branch Rickey and Jackie Robinson on the day Robinson signed a contract to play for the Dodgers

the color bar? Many players doubted it. Buck Leonard said, "We didn't think he was going to get there. We thought we had other ballplayers who were better ballplayers than he."[20] Cleveland Indians ace Bob Feller, who frequently pitched exhibition games versus black players, said Robinson "couldn't hit an inside pitch to save his neck."[21]

Some Negro leaguers thought a proven superstar like Paige or Gibson would be the best person to lead the way into the majors. Most favored a younger star like the Newark Eagles' Monte Irvin. Eagles owner Effa Manley said that "Monte . . . was the choice of all Negro National and American League club owners as the number one player to join a white major league team. We all agreed . . . he was the best qualified by temperament, ability, sense of loyalty, morals, age, experience, and physique."[22]

Rickey, nonetheless, chose Jackie Robinson. He decided to sign Robinson to a contract with the Montreal Royals of the International League, because he believed that Canadians harbored less racial prejudice than American fans. Robinson signed a contract with the Dodgers October 23, 1945, in Montreal.

Many black players did not particularly like Robinson. But once he was signed, they did all they could to help him. As Cool Papa Bell said, "If he missed his chance, I don't know how long we'd go before we'd get another."[23]

Given his chance, Robinson made the most of it. He led the league in 1946 with .349 batting and .985 fielding averages, tied for the league lead with 113 runs scored, finished second with 40 stolen bases, and was named the league's Most Valuable Player. Clearly, Jackie Robinson would be wearing a Brooklyn Dodger uniform in 1947.

One of the Negro leagues' mightiest figures would never witness that sight. On New Year's Day of 1943, Josh Gibson had fallen into a coma. He recovered, but doctors told him he had a brain tumor that should be removed. He refused the brain surgery.

Gibson went to his mother's house on January 20, 1947, and told her he was going to die that night. He went to bed and gathered his family and trophies around him. Gibson's sister, Annie Mahaffey, described what happened at about 10:30 P.M.: "We were all laughing and talking, and then he had a stroke. He just got through laughing and then he raised up in the bed and went to talk, but you couldn't understand what he was saying. Then he lay back down and died right off."[24]

Chapter 10

"WE PAVED THE WAY"

During a 1947 exhibition game, Dodger manager Leo Durocher passed out a simple announcement to the press box. It read, "The Brooklyn Dodgers today purchased the contract of Jackie Roosevelt Robinson from the Montreal Royals. He will report immediately. Branch Rickey."[1] Jackie Robinson was now a major leaguer.

It was no easy transition to the majors. Five Dodgers, including shortstop Pee Wee Reese, objected to the signing. Some National League players even threatened a strike if Robinson appeared in a game. Given the past actions and statements of baseball officials, National League president Ford Frick's response was surprisingly quick and forceful. He commented:

> I do not care if half the league strikes. Those who do will encounter quick retribution. All will be suspended, and I don't care if it wrecks the National League for five years. This is the United States of America, and one citizen has as much right to play as another. The National League will go up and down the line with Robinson, no matter what the consequences.[2]

Once Robinson started playing, fears of fan and player unrest subsided quickly. Pee Wee Reese became one of his leading defenders. When Philadelphia Phillies players taunted Robinson, Reese and teammate Duke Snider threatened a fight. The Phillies stopped their harassment.

Fans flocked to see Robinson. Among them was 79-year-old retired ballplayer and baseball historian Sol White, the link between presegregation and postsegregation days. Black and white fans alike applauded Robinson's timely hitting and daring baserunning. One of them, Paul Binder, recalled, "It felt uncomfortable in the first game and a little awkward in the second game. By the third game we were all cheering wildly together and spilling soda on each other. By May there weren't any black fans and white fans, just Dodger fans."[3]

Jackie Robinson was only the first of many black ballplayers to enter the major leagues. The Cleveland Indians, now owned by Bill Veeck, signed Larry Doby. Don Newcombe and Roy Campanella joined Dodger farm teams and soon entered the majors. Monte Irvin became a New York Giant.

Not all black entries into the big leagues proved successful. Willard Brown and Hank Thompson played briefly with the St. Louis Browns in 1947. After continuous taunts from St. Louis fans, both quit the team and returned to the Kansas City Monarchs. Brown, less than impressed with the St. Louis American League team, later said, "The Browns couldn't beat the Monarchs no way, only if we was all asleep."[4]

Major-league signings of black players aroused pride in blacks, but one player's signing turned pride into elation. Robinson, Doby, and the others were young stars. Satchel Paige was a legend, as colorful and heroic as Babe Ruth was to the white major leagues.

Veeck signed him with the Indians in July 1948. Critics claimed that Veeck, who was known for his showmanship, signed Paige only as a publicity stunt. Granted, Paige drew crowds. But the Indians owner knew the 40-plus-year-old hurler still had unhittable stuff and could be helpful in the Indians' pennant race.

Whatever the reason Veeck signed Paige, the famed pitcher did indeed draw crowds. Veeck recalled Paige's first start, against the White Sox in Comiskey Park:

How could I forget that game! According to the records Satch drew 51,103, the largest crowd ever to see a night game at Comiskey Park. But in point of fact there were probably 70,000 people there.

The crowd was so great they simply burst through police lines like a tidal wave and swamped the turnstiles. They were jammed together so tightly underneath the stands that it was impossible for them to leave, even if they wanted to. And nobody wanted to, that's for sure.

I didn't even get a seat, it was so crowded. I got tickets for Sidney Schiff, one of my partners, who came in with a group. . . . I noticed Schiff and the group crouched against the railings far from the seats they were supposed to have. I asked, "What are you doing here? Why aren't you in your seats?" Schiff said, "Joe Louis and a group of his friends are in our seats, and I'm not about to fight him for them."[5]

The importance of the game hardly fazed the famous pitcher. While other Indians pitchers were running in the outfield before the game, Paige was reading a newspaper. Someone asked him, "Ain't you gonna run, ain't you gonna get in shape?" Paige responded, "No, where I come from we throw the ball across the plate, we don't carry it across."[6]

Paige was more than equal to the occasion. Veeck said, "He did all that could be expected right from the start. He was in control all the way in that game, with his assortment of fastballs, hesitation pitches and 'bat dodgers.' He threw overhand and three quarters and he kept the Sox popping up. He didn't walk a man all night. All the Sox could get off him were five singles."[7]

More than 200,000 fans witnessed Paige's first three major-league starts. A game on August 20, 1948, drew 78,382 fans to Cleveland's Municipal

Stadium, then the largest night game crowd in history. Paige responded by tossing a shutout. He won six games in 1948, losing only one, and became the first black pitcher to appear in a major-league World Series.

Robinson and Paige were not the only players from the Negro leagues to achieve stardom in the majors. From the late 1940s until the early 1960s, the Most Valuable Player awards were dominated by Negro-league alumni. Jackie Robinson (1949), Roy Campanella (1951, 1953, 1955), Willie Mays (1954 and 1965), Don Newcombe (1956), Hank Aaron (1957), Ernie Banks (1958 and 1959), and Elston Howard (1963) all won MVP trophies. Larry Doby finished a close second in the American League Most Valuable Player balloting in 1954.

Some Negro-league stars received invitations to the majors too late in their careers. Monarchs pitcher Hilton Smith was afraid he would be assigned to the minor leagues and forced to take a pay cut. For others, it was a matter of pride. Buck Leonard and Cool Papa Bell were both asked by Veeck to play with the Browns when he bought the team in 1951. Both declined. Leonard explained, "I was too old, past my prime, and didn't want to embarrass anyone or hurt the chances of those who might follow."[8]

Some Negro-league stars made brief appearances in the majors. Quincy Trouppe, who had rejected a scout's suggestion that he go to Cuba and learn Spanish so he could pass as a Cuban, played in a handful of games with the 1952 Indians. He had lost most of the skills that made him a fixture behind the plate in the East-West game. But years later he could point with pride to a line in the baseball encyclopedias:

	AB	R	H	2B	3B	HR	RBI	BA
Trouppe, Quincy	10	1	1	0	0	0	0	.00

Perhaps the saddest story belonged to Ray Dandridge, a slick-fielding third baseman. Roy Campanella said, "I played with Billy Cox and I saw Brooks Robinson and a lot of other great third basemen. Believe me, Dan-

Ray Dandridge

dridge could match them all."[9] Dandridge, at 36, was offered a contract with the International League's Minneapolis Millers, a New York Giants farm team. He terrorized IL pitchers and gave invaluable instructions to a young roommate named Willie Mays. Even though he was named IL Rookie of the Year in 1949 and Most Valuable Player the following season, the Giants never called him up to the majors. Giants owner Horace Stoneham told Dandridge he was kept in the minors because he was "the drawing power of Minneapolis."[10] Years later Dandridge commented, "I just wanted to put my left foot in [a major-league park]. I just would have liked to have been up there one day, even if it was only to get a cup of coffee."[11]

Baseball has always been more than a sport. It has been a great influence on American life. Just as baseball's exclusion of blacks in the 1890s was part of the atmosphere that permitted a Supreme Court decision allowing segregation, so was Jackie Robinson's entry to the majors in 1947 a major step in the process of what would become a civil rights revolution. President Harry S Truman soon afterward issued an order ending segregation in the armed forces. The Supreme Court in 1954 declared school segregation unconstitutional. Congress passed laws that called for the integration of restaurants, hotels, and other public accommodations. Segregated institutions were becoming a thing of the past—including the Negro leagues.

Two circumstances led to the Negro leagues' downfall. First, major-league owners signed star players with little or no compensation to their Negro-league teams. Rickey dismissed his luring of top black players by claiming the Negro leagues were run by racketeers. "They are not leagues and have no right to expect organized baseball to respect them," Rickey said.[12]

Negro-league owners were caught defenseless by the raids. They dared not challenge the major leagues. After all, the main purpose of their teams had always been to prepare players for the day when the majors would accept them. Monarchs owner J. L. Wilkinson received not one penny in compensation for Jackie Robinson. Yet he said, "I am very glad to see Jackie get this chance."[13]

When asked how much money she got for her Eagles superstars, Effa Manley laughed and replied that Rickey "didn't even answer our letters when we wrote him about Newcombe, let alone give us anything. He knew we were in no position to challenge him. The fans would never have forgiven us. We got nothing for Newcombe, $5,000 for Monte Irvin, and $15,000 for Doby. That's all."[14]

The main cause of the Negro leagues' collapse was integration. Black fans had waited at least a lifetime to see their players in organized baseball alongside whites. Once that dream was achieved, all-black baseball no longer seemed meaningful.

Even the best black teams were abandoned. A stunned J. L. Wilkinson watched as buses of onetime Kansas City Monarchs fans traveled hundreds of miles to see Jackie Robinson in St. Louis. Why watch the Eagles without Larry Doby when you could watch Jackie Robinson in Brooklyn or Larry Doby when the Indians came to New York? Newark attendance sank from 120,000 in 1946 to 57,000 in 1947 to 35,000 in 1948. Buck Leonard's Homestead Grays faced similar problems. "We'd get three hundred people to a game," he said. "We couldn't even draw flies."[15]

The East-West all-star game continued to draw well in the first years of integration. After all, this was a chance to see future major leaguers in action. But when black players started appearing in the major-league all-star games, black fans saw the Chicago event as a second-rate product and attendance plummeted.

Gradually, the teams fell. Cum Posey died in 1946, and the once-proud Homestead Grays disbanded in 1948. New York's Black Yankees also folded after the season. The Eagles were sold, moved to Houston, and collapsed soon afterward. Wilkinson, now 74 years old, sold the Monarchs and retired. Gus Greenlee died, and Greenlee Field was razed in 1948.

The Negro National League disbanded in 1948, with some clubs joining remaining Negro American League teams. By 1953 only four teams were left in the NAL. This skeleton of a league carried on until 1960, then died without a whimper.

The Negro leagues were gone but not forgotten by those who had endured endless bus rides and lunch meat sandwiches for the opportunity to play first-class baseball and wait until the major leagues would accept them as equals. Jackie Robinson said of the Negro leagues, "For me, it turned out to be a pretty miserable way to make a buck."[16] He recalled "low salaries, sloppy umpiring, and questionable business connections of many of the team owners."[17] Effa Manley responded to Robinson's criticisms in a magazine article by writing, "No greater ingratitude was ever displayed."[18]

Most of the players, although wishing the major leagues' color barrier had been broken earlier, said they appreciated the Negro-league experience. New York Cubans pitcher Pat Scantlebury commented:

> I wanted to play, and I could only play in the black leagues so I played in the black leagues. I always felt, after integration, that our efforts, all those games and all those bus rides, made it possible for Jackie Robinson and others who followed. Yes, sir, we paved the way.[19]

Thousands gathered at Cooperstown in 1966 for Ted Williams's Hall of Fame acceptance speech. He surprised the audience when he said, "I hope that some day Satchel Paige and Josh Gibson will be voted into the Hall of Fame as symbols of the great Negro players who are not here only because they were not given the chance."[20]

Five years later the Hall of Fame appointed a special Committee on Negro Leagues to honor some of those black stars. In 1971 Satchel Paige became the first Negro-league player honored. Buck Leonard recalled:

> I was in Cooperstown the day Satchel Paige was inducted, and I stayed awake almost all night that night thinking about it. You know, a day like that stays with you a long time. It's something you never had any dream you'd ever see. Like men walking on the moon. I always wanted to go up there to Cooperstown. You felt like you had a reason, because it's the home of baseball, but you never had a *special* reason. We never thought we'd get in the Hall of Fame. It was so far from us, we didn't even consider it, we didn't even think it would someday come to reality. We thought the way we were playing was the way it was going to continue. I never had any dream it would come. But that night I felt like I was part of it at last.[21]

The following season, Leonard had even more of a reason to be proud. He and Josh Gibson joined Paige in baseball's hallowed Hall. In the next 11 seasons, Monte Irvin, Cool Papa Bell, Judy Johnson, Oscar Charleston, John Henry Lloyd, Martin DiHigo, Rube Foster, and Ray Dandridge joined them.

No Negro-league stars have been enshrined in recent years, although players and fans insist dozens of others deserve the honor. Perhaps in future years Smokey Joe Williams, Cannonball Redding, Cristobal Torriente, Jose Mendez, Bingo DeMoss, Ted Page, Turkey Stearnes, Mule Suttles, Cum Posey, J. L. Wilkinson, Effa Manley, Willie Wells, Bullet Joe Rogan, and Double Duty Radcliffe will join the Ruths, Speakers, Cobbs, Aarons, Fellers, Deans, Paiges, and Charlestons in baseball's most elite society.

A baseball generation after Jackie Robinson entered the major leagues, former Negro-league players' minds were utilized as little as their bodies were before Robinson joined the Dodgers. There were a few exceptions: Judy Johnson scouted for the Philadelphia Athletics and Phillies; and Cool Papa Bell, as a scout, signed Ernie Banks for the Cubs. But it was not until 1961 that former Kansas City Monarch Buck O'Neil joined the Chicago Cubs as the first black major-league coach.

Another baseball generation would pass before Frank Robinson became the first black major-league manager, taking the reins of the Cleveland Indians in 1975. Others joined him. Their leadership skills became recognized. In 1989 Frank Robinson, now with the Baltimore Orioles, was named American League Manager of the Year. Clarence "Cito" Gaston managed the Toronto Blue Jays to World Series championships in 1992 and 1993.

Somewhere, Rube Foster must be smiling.

NOTES

Chapter 1

1. Anthony J. O'Connor, *Baseball for the Love of It: Hall of Famers Tell It Like It Was* (New York: Macmillan, 1982), p. 272.
2. Donn Rogosin, *Invisible Men: Life in Baseball's Negro Leagues* (New York: Atheneum, 1983), p. 84.
3. Ibid., p. 7.

Chapter 2

1. Robert Peterson, *Only the Ball Was White: A History of the Legendary Black Players and All-Black Professional Teams* (New York: Oxford University Press, 1970), p. 16.
2. Peter Levine, *A. G. Spalding and the Rise of Baseball* (New York: Oxford University Press, 1985), p. 47.
3. Peterson, p. 23.
4. Ibid., p. 26.
5. Michael L. Cooper, *Playing America's Game: The Story of Negro League Baseball* (New York: Lodestar, 1993), p. 9.
6. John Holway, *Blackball Stars: Negro League Pioneers* (Westport, Conn.: Meckler, 1988), p. 2.
7. Levine, p. 47.
8. Peterson, p. 28.
9. Ibid., p. 54.
10. Lee Allen, *The American League Story* (New York: Hill and Wang, 1965), pp. 21–22.
11. Sol White, *History of Colored Baseball*, quoted in Holway, *Blackball Stars*, p. 1.

Chapter 3

1. Charles Alexander, *Our Game: An American Baseball History* (New York: Henry Holt, 1991), p. 153.
2. Lowell Reidenbaugh, *Baseball's Hall of Fame: Cooperstown, Where the Legends Live* (St. Louis: Sporting News, 1986), p. 82.
3. Mike Shatzkin, ed., *The Ballplayers* (New York: Arbor House, 1990), p. 1133.
4. Holway, *Blackball Stars*, p. 61.
5. Ibid., p. 20.
6. Rogosin, p. 93.
7. Dan Gutman, *Baseball Babylon* (New York: Penguin, 1992), p. 240.
8. Bruce Chadwick, *When the Game Was Black and White: The Illustrated History of Baseball's Negro Leagues* (New York: Abbeville Press, 1993), p. 34.

Chapter 4

1. Peterson, p. 125.
2. Ibid., p. 128.
3. Chadwick, p. 54.
4. Rogosin, p. 22.
5. O'Connor, p. 208.
6. John Holway, *Voices from the Great Black Baseball Leagues* (New York: Dodd, Mead, 1975), p. 258.
7. Rogosin, p. 128.
8. Chadwick, p. 119.
9. Ibid., p. 65.
10. Holway, *Voices from the Great Black Baseball Leagues*, p. 151.
11. Rogosin, p. 79.
12. Holway, *Blackball Stars*, p. 319.
13. Chadwick, p. 68.
14. Peterson, pp. 124–125.

15. Chadwick, p. 79.
16. Interview with Ted Radcliffe, January 26, 1993.
17. Rogosin, p. 73.
18. Chadwick, p. 56.
19. Paul Dickson, *Baseball's Greatest Quotations* (New York: HarperCollins, 1991), p. 38.
20. "Only the Ball Was White," WTTW-TV, Chicago, aired March 14, 1980.
21. Rogosin, p. 68.
22. Janet Bruce, *The Kansas City Monarchs: Champions of Black Baseball* (Lawrence, Kans.: University Press of Kansas, 1985), p. 40.
23. Holway, *Blackball Stars*, p. 163.
24. Rogosin, p. 66.

Chapter 5
1. Peterson, p. 131.
2. Holway, *Voices from the Great Black Baseball Leagues*, p. 236.
3. Cooper, p. 40.
4. Dickson, p. 105.
5. Chadwick, p. 124.
6. Shatzkin, p. 840.
7. Holway, *Voices from the Great Black Baseball Leagues*, p. 340.
8. Chadwick, p. 124.
9. Peterson, p. 140.
10. Dickson, p. 333.
11. Joel Zoss and John Bowman, *Diamonds in the Rough: The Untold History of Baseball* (New York: Macmillan, 1989), p. 213.
12. Rogosin, pp. 97–98.
13. Ibid., p. 168.
14. Chadwick, p. 146.
15. O'Connor, p. 209.
16. Peterson, pp. 143–144.

Chapter 6
1. Holway, *Blackball Stars*, p. 100.
2. Ibid.
3. Ibid., p. 97.
4. Rogosin, p. 12.
5. Eric Nadel and Craig R. Wright, *The Man Who Stole First Base: Tales from Baseball's Past* (Dallas: Taylor, 1989), p. 78.
6. Reidenbaugh, p. 43.
7. L. Robert Davis, ed., *Insider's Baseball* (New York: Scribner's, 1982), p. 110.
8. Holway, *Voices from the Great Black Baseball Leagues*, p. 110.
9. Reidenbaugh, p. 24.
10. Craig Carter, *Daguerreotypes*, 8th ed. (St. Louis: Sporting News, 1990), p. 24.
11. Ibid.
12. Holway, *Blackball Stars*, p. 150.
13. Ibid., p. 237.
14. Reidenbaugh, p. 69.
15. Peterson, p. 160.

Chapter 7
1. Cooper, p. 52.
2. Holway, *Blackball Stars*, p. 336.
3. Bruce, p. 24.
4. Rogosin, p. 103.
5. Holway, *Blackball Stars*, p. 310.
6. Rogosin, p. 14.
7. Ibid., p. 106.

Chapter 8
1. Holway, *Blackball Stars*, p. xii.
2. Cooper, p. 18.
3. Interview with Ted Radcliffe, January 27, 1993.
4. Holway, *Voices from the Great Black Baseball Leagues*, p. 194.

5. Chadwick, p. 75.
6. Carter, p. 164.
7. Ibid., p. 165.
8. Holway, *Blackball Stars*, p. 147.
9. Cooper, p. 135.
10. Ibid., p. 49.
11. Rogosin, p. 174.
12. Shatzkin, p. 351.
13. Ibid., p. 533.
14. Ibid., p. 285.
15. Carter, p. 103.
16. O'Connor, p. 210.
17. Holway, *Voices from the Great Black Baseball Leagues*, p. 235.

Chapter 9
1. Chadwick, p. 98.
2. Bruce, p. 88.
3. "Only the Ball Was White," WTTW-TV, Chicago, aired March 14, 1980.
4. Cooper, p. 61.
5. Rogosin, p. 181.
6. Chadwick, p. 156.
7. Rogosin, p. 190.
8. Chadwick, p. 157.
9. Holway, *Voices from the Great Black Baseball Leagues*, p. 252.
10. Ibid., p. 10.
11. Dickson, p. 143.
12. Gutman, pp. 334–335.
13. Ibid., p. 334.
14. Holway, *Voices from the Great Black Baseball Leagues*, p. 13.
15. Ibid., p. 14.
16. Peterson, p. 187.
17. Rogosin, p. 208.
18. Ibid., p. 201.
19. Peterson, p. 190.
20. Ibid., p. 193.
21. Red Barber, *1947: When All Hell Broke Loose in Baseball* (Garden City, N.Y.: Doubleday, 1982), p. 52.
22. Carter, p. 133.
23. Rogosin, p. 85.
24. Peterson, p. 168.

Chapter 10
1. Barber, p. 130.
2. Dickson, p. 143.
3. Chadwick, p. 169.
4. Shatzkin, p. 127.
5. Bill Veeck, "The Game I'll Never Forget," in *Baseball Digest: 50 Years of Baseball,* ed. John Kuenster (Evanston, Ill.: Century, 1992), p. 73.
6. Reidenbaugh, p. 206.
7. Veeck, p. 73.
8. Carter, p. 163.
9. Ibid., p. 71.
10. Daniel Oknent and Steve Wolf, *Baseball Anecdotes* (New York: Harper & Row, 1989), p. 187.
11. Rogosin, p. 21.
12. Neil J. Sullivan, *The Minors* (New York: St. Martin's Press, 1990), p. 202.
13. Alexander, p. 200.
14. Holway, *Voices from the Great Black Baseball Leagues*, p. 317.
15. Holway, *Blackball Stars*, p. 326.
16. Rogosin, p. 179.
17. Ibid., p. 204.
18. Holway, *Voices from the Great Black Baseball Leagues*, p. 316.
19. Chadwick, p. 79.
20. Zoss and Bowman, p. 154.
21. Holway, *Voices from the Great Black Baseball Leagues*, p. 271.

FOR FURTHER READING

Alexander, Charles. *John McGraw.* New York: Viking, 1988.

———. *Our Game: An American Baseball History.* New York: Henry Holt, 1991.

———. *Ty Cobb.* New York: Oxford University Press, 1984.

Barber, Red. *1947: When All Hell Broke Loose in Baseball.* Garden City, N.Y.: Doubleday, 1982.

Bruce, Janet. *The Kansas City Monarchs: Champions of Black Baseball.* Lawrence, Kans.: University Press of Kansas, 1985.

Carter, Craig. *Daguerreotypes.* 8th ed. St. Louis: Sporting News, 1990.

Chadwick, Bruce. *When the Game Was Black and White: The Illustrated History of Baseball's Negro Leagues.* New York: Abbeville Press, 1993.

Cooper, Michael L. *Playing America's Game: The Story of Negro League Baseball.* New York: Lodestar, 1993.

Davis, L. Robert, ed. *Insiders' Baseball.* New York: Scribner's, 1982.

Dickson, Paul. *Baseball's Greatest Quotations.* New York: HarperCollins, 1991.

Gardner, Robert, and Dennis Shortelle. *The Forgotten Players: The Story of Black Baseball in America.* New York: Walker and Company, 1993.

Grossman, James R. *Land of Hope: Chicago, Black Southerners, and the Great Migration.* Chicago: University of Chicago Press, 1989.

Gutman, Dan. *Baseball Babylon.* New York: Penguin, 1992.

Holway, John. *Blackball Stars: Negro League Pioneers.* Westport, Conn.: Meckler, 1988.

———. *Voices from the Great Black Baseball Leagues.* New York: Dodd, Mead, 1975.

Kuenster, John, ed. *Baseball Digest: 50 Years of Baseball.* Evanston, Ill.: Century, 1992.

Levine, Peter. *A. G. Spalding and the Rise of Baseball.* New York: Oxford University Press, 1985.

Lowrey, Philip J. *Green Cathedrals.* Reading, Mass.: Addison-Wesley, 1992.

Nadel, Eric, and Craig R. Wright. *The Man Who Stole First Base: Tales from Baseball's Past.* Dallas: Taylor, 1989.

O'Connor, Anthony J. *Baseball for the Love of It: Hall of Famers Tell It Like It Was.* New York: Macmillan, 1982.

Oknent, Daniel, and Steve Wolf. *Baseball Anecdotes.* New York: Harper & Row, 1989.

Peterson, Robert. *Only the Ball Was White: A History of the Legendary Black Players and All-Black Professional Teams.* New York: Oxford University Press, 1970.

Reidenbaugh, Lowell. *Baseball's Hall of Fame: Cooperstown, Where the Legends Live.* St. Louis: Sporting News, 1986.

Rogosin, Donn. *Invisible Men: Life in Baseball's Negro Leagues.* New York: Atheneum, 1983.

Shatzkin, Mike, ed. *The Ballplayers.* New York: Arbor House, 1990.

Sullivan, Neil J. *The Minors.* New York: St. Martin's Press, 1990.

Zoss, Joel, and John Bowman. *Diamonds in the Rough: The Untold History of Baseball.* New York: Macmillan, 1989.

INDEX

Aaron, Hank, 85
All Nations League, 26
Almeida, Rafael, 66
American League, 19, 75
American Association, 14, 18
American Negro League, 56
Anson, Adrian "Cap," 13, 14, 16–17
Atlantic City Bachrach Giants, 28, 30

Baltimore Black Sox, 28, 59
Baltimore Elite Giants, 32, 35, 39, 72
Baltimore Orioles, 19, 90
Bankhead, Sam, 59
Banks, Ernie, 85, 90
Barnes, Virgil, 26
Bassett, Lloyd "Pepper," 39
Bell, James "Cool Papa," 9, 24, 39, 49–50, 59, 63, 68, 72, 80, . 85, 89, 90
Benson, Gene, 62
Biot, Charlie, 39
Birmingham Black Barons, 10, 59
Black, Joe, 35–36
Breadon, Sam, 75
Brooklyn Brown Dodge, 76, 80
Brooklyn Dodgers, 32, 74, 76, 77, 83
Brooklyn Royal Giants, 18, 28
Brown, Willard, 83

Calloway, Cab, 70
Campanella, Roy, 32, 72, 83, 85
Chandler, Albert "Happy," 75, 77
Charleston, Oscar, 9, 25, 28, 48–49, 58, 59, 89
Chicago American Giants, 24, 25, 26, 27, 28, 30, 35, 36, 59, 68
Chicago Columbia Giants, 18, 19
Chicago Cubs, 23-24, 26, 90
Chicago Giants, 27
Chicago Leland Giants, 22, 23–24
Chicago Unions, 18
Chicago White Sox, 19, 26, 27, 68
Chicago White Stockings, 13, 14, 16
Cincinnati Red Stockings, 13, 18, 27
Cincinnati Reds, 57, 62, 66

Ciudad Trujillo, 45
Civil War, 12
Cleveland Indians, 42, 46, 79, 83, 90
Cobb, Ty, 48, 65
Columbus Blue Birds, 59
Comiskey, Charles, 19, 24
Comiskey, Grace, 68
Cornelius, William "Sug," 43, 68
Cox, William, 75, 85
Crutchfield, Jimmy, 51, 59
Cuban Giants, 18
Cuban Stars, 27
Cuban X Giants, 18

Dandridge, Ray, 67, 75, 85–86, 89
Dayton Marcos, 27
Dean, Dizzy, 43–44, 46, 63, 73
DeMoss, Elwood "Bingo," 25, 90
Detroit Stars, 27, 59
Detroit Tigers, 65, 67
Didrickson, Babe, 56
DiHigo, Martin, 51–52, 89
DiMaggio, Joe, 64, 72
Dixon, Rap, 59, 63
Doby, Larry, 72, 73, 85, 87
Donaldson, John, 26, 67
Drake, Bill, 26
Durocher, Leo, 74, 82

East-West all star game, 70–71, 87
Eastern Colored League, 28, 56
Ewing, Buck, 54

Feller, Bob, 46, 63, 72, 79
Fields, Wilmer, 66, 73
Foster, Andrew "Rube," 22–30, 56, 62, 89
Foster, Bill, 63, 67
Fowler, John "Bud," 14
Frick, Ford, 74, 75, 82

Gaston, Clarence "Cito," 90
Gatewood, Bob, 50
Gehrig, Lou, 52, 53, 60, 73
Gehringer, Charlie, 67
Gibson, Josh, 9, 45, 53–54, 58, 59, 60, 63, 64, 67, 72, 73, 75, 79, 80, 89
Grant, Charlie, 19–20
Grant, Frank, 16

Greenberg, Hank, 72
Greenlee, W. A. "Gus," 58–60, 70, 88
Greenlee Field, 59, 88
Griffith, Clark, 73
Griffith Stadium, 54

Hall of Fame, 89
Harnett, Gay, 73
Harridge, Will, 75
Havana Cuban Stars, 28
Homestead Grays, 36, 39, 43, 50, 51, 53, 54, 58, 59, 60, 66, 73, 87, 88
House of David, 56
Howard, Elston, 85
Hughes, Sammy T., 40

Indianapolis ABCs, 27, 28
Indianapolis Athletics, 59
International League, 16, 17, 19, 80, 86
Irvin, Monte, 9, 44, 50, 72, 79, 83, 87, 89

Jackson, Rufus "Sonnyland," 60
Jim Crow laws, 19, 44
Johnson, Byron "Ban", 22, 30
Johnson, Grant "Home Run," 23, 65
Johnson, Walter, 49, 67
Johnson, William Julius "Judy," 28, 34, 40, 50–51, 54, 58, 59, 67, 89, 90

Kansas City Blues, 63
Kansas City Monarchs, 27, 28, 33, 35, 40, 46, 56, 57–58, 59, 63, 78, 83, 88, 90
Ku Klux Klan, 38, 49

Landis, Kenesaw Mountain, 10, 22, 27-28, 62–63, 74, 75
Latin American teams, 65-68
Leland, Frank, 23
Leonard, Walter "Buck," 9, 10, 33, 34, 37, 40, 52–53, 60, 72, 73, 75, 79, 85, 87
Lloyd, John Henry, 22, 25, 65–66, 89
Louis, Joe, 70
Luque, Adolfo, 66

Mack, Connie, 67
Malarcher, Dave, 36, 63
Manley, Effa, 33, 79, 87, 88, 90
Manning, Max, 66, 70
Marsans, Armando, 66
Marshall, Jack, 38
Mathewson, Christy,22
Mays, Willie, 9, 10, 85, 86
McDonald, Webster, 63
McDuffie,Terris, 77
McGinnity, Joe, 22
McGraw, John, 19-20, 22, 30, 67
McPhail, Larry, 75
Memphis Red Sox, 59
Mendez, Jose, 26, 28, 62, 63, 66, 90
Minneapolis Millers, 86
Montreal Royals, 8, 80, 82
Morton, C. H., 14
Most Valuable Player awards, 85, 86
Mulane, Tony, 16

Nashville Elite Giants, 59
Nation, Carrie, 26
National Association of Base Ball Players, 12
National Association of Professional Baseball Players, 13
Negro American League, 60, 79, 88
National League, 13, 18, 74, 75, 82
Negro National League, 27, 28, 30, 53, 56, 59, 60, 79, 88
Newark Eagles, 9, 33, 66, 70, 72, 79
Newark Little Giants, 16
Newcombe, Don, 72, 83, 85, 87
New York Giants, 9, 17, 22, 26, 62, 67, 83
New York Lincoln Giants, 25, 28
New York Yankees, 62, 64, 72
night games, 57
Northwestern League, 14

O'Neil, John "Buck," 35, 40, 90
Owens, Jesse, 49, 70

Page, Ted, 36, 48, 49, 51, 59, 60, 63, 90
Paige, Leroy "Satchel," 34, 42–46, 50, 59, 60, 63, 64, 71, 72, 75, 79, 83-85, 89
Partee, Ray, 50
Petway, Bruce, 65
Philadelphia Athletics, 22, 62, 67, 90
Philadelphia Giants, 18
Philadelphia Hilldales, 28, 51
Philadelphia Phillies, 62, 74, 82
Pittsburgh Crawfords, 36, 43, 45, 50, 51, 59, 60, 63, 64
Pittsburgh Pirates, 50
Philadelphia Stars, 22, 62
Plessy v. Ferguson, 19
Poles, Spotswood, 25, 63
Posey, Cumberland "Cum," 58–59, 60, 88, 90
Powell, Jake, 73

racism, 12-20, 32–40, 49, 62–63
Radcliffe, Ted "Double Duty," 38–39, 59, 63, 90
Redding, Dick "Cannonball," 25, 36, 89
Renfroe, Othello, 4
Reese, Pee Wee, 82
Rickey, Branch, 75-80, 82, 87
Robinson, Frank, 90
Robinson, Jack Roosevelt (Jackie), 8, 78–80, 82, 83, 85, 86, 88, 90
Rogan, Wilbur "Bullet Joe," 35, 51, 90
Russell, Johnny, 59
Ruth, Babe, 48, 49, 51, 53, 60, 66, 83
Ryan, Nolan, 44

St. Louis Browns, 75, 83
St. Louis Cardinals, 43, 75, 76
St. Louis Giants, 27
St. Louis Stars, 50, 59
Scantlebury, Pat, 88
Schorling, John, 24
Smith, Hilton, 58, 85
Smith, Theolic, 67
Southern Negro Leagues, 33, 56
Speaker, Tris, 48, 49, 65
Stearnes, Norman "Turkey," 35, 90

Stephens, Jake, 59
Stoneham, Horace, 86
Stovey, George, 16, 17
Streeter, Sam, 25
Strong, Nat, 28
Suttles, George "Mule," 63, 90

Thomas, Dave "Showboat," 77
Thompson, Hank, 83
Toledo Blue Stockings, 14, 15–16
Toronto Blue Jays, 90
Torriente, Cristobal, 66, 90
Traynor, Pie, 50, 73
Trouppe, Quincy, 67, 85
Trujillo, Rafael, 45, 60

United States League, 76, 78

Veeck, Bill, 42, 74–75, 77, 83, 85

Waddell, Rube, 22, 62
Wagner, Honus, 22, 65
Walker, Weldy Wilburforce, 14, 15
Walker, Moses Fleetwood "Fleet," 14, 15–16, 18
Waner, Paul, 73
Washington Senators, 49, 73
Wells, Willie, 40, 63, 75, 90
White, Sol, 16, 20, 83
Wilkinson, J. L., 26, 27, 46, 56-57, 60, 87, 90
Williams, Joe "Smokey Joe" or "Cyclone Joe," 5, 58, 62, 63, 89
Williams, Ted, 72, 89
Wilson, Jud, 59
World Series (Negro leagues), 28–30, 60
Wright, Richard, 58
Wrigley, Phillip, 75

Yawley, Tom, 75
Young, Cy, 44